Prayer Chain

Prayer Chain

Scott Lazenby

Prayer Chain

© Scott Lazenby 2018

This book is a work of fiction. Named locations are used fictitiously, and characters and incidents are the product of the author's imagination. Any resemblance to actual events or places or persons, living or dead, is entirely coincidental.

Published by
Lighthouse Christian Publishing
SAN 257-4330
5531 Dufferin Drive
Savage, Minnesota, 55378
United States of America

www.lighthousechristianpublishing.com

1

The first clue was the rain. A fine drizzle was so much a part of life in the west Cascades that people scarcely noticed its presence. They refused to carry umbrellas, letting the mist cover their hair in a light spray and their clothes in dampness. Oregonians seemed to like their air with fizz.

An occasional shower was normal, too, where a person had to run from a shop or home to a parked car, cursing the time it took to fumble for a key.

But this was something else. It had rained hard, almost without pause, for over a month. The creeks and rivers were swollen, flooding the lowest homes. The strawberry crop was ruined—berries that had not succumbed to mold and rot were devoured by slugs escaping the wet mud. The Cedar Creek Youth Soccer League had cancelled its season when the fields turned into lakes.

At the time, though, Nancy Mackay wasn't looking for clues. Squeezed under the rafters of a musty attic, she was looking for a leak. She inched along, keeping her knees on the joists to avoid breaking through the plaster ceiling. Fine particles of dust and insulation shimmered in the beam of her flashlight, and her neck and wrists were beginning to itch. She sneezed, raising a cloud of dust.

When she finally reached what she thought was the right spot, she ran the flashlight over the tongue-and-groove roof boards. Except for a few damp spots at the joints, she saw nothing. She imagined as much as felt a wet spot on her back, and she twisted her body to look directly overhead, hoping to see a steady drip or at least a rivulet running down a rafter. But the dim light of the flashlight revealed no evidence. She sneezed again, then backed out to the access hatch at the other end of the attic.

In the main room of the café, Nancy brushed the dust off her jeans and turtleneck shirt, and stared at the light bulb in the center of the ceiling. Water was seeping down the side of the fixture and gathering at the end of the bulb before falling in a steady drip. There was already a half inch of water in the bucket she had put under the leak when she discovered it. So where was it coming from?

A foot from the light, a bulge was forming in the ceiling paint. She shrugged and dragged a phone book from a pile of papers stacked under the counter.

"Roof Riders!" the man's voice on the phone said.

"Hi. I own a restaurant, and I've got a leak somewhere in the roof."

"Well, we can fix it. We can have someone out there by 3:00—"

"By 3:00? Your ad says that you can handle any problem at any time of day or night."

"Oh, that's true! We can handle _your_ problem at

3:00. And we'll be fixing roofs all day. If you look outside, you might see it's raining. Been doing that for a while."

"Yes, I've noticed."

She gave him her name and address, and began busying herself with the tasks of opening the café.

***

"It's open, Mary!" She beckoned through the plate glass window at Mary Mowatt, her head cook, who, huddling close to the building to escape the rain, was fishing in her purse for the key.

Mary's shoulders fell in relief, and she darted through the door into the warmth of the café. "Thanks Nancy, I didn't know you were here, didn't see your car. I got soaked to the bone just walking from the bus stop."

"Well, hang up that wet coat, and I'll get us some coffee; it should be brewed by now. I decided to walk in from home today, rain and all. Wasn't so bad with an umbrella and gum boots...but I think I got some strange looks from a few drivers."

As she tipped the coffee pot, Nancy paused to breathe in the strong, slightly sweet aroma. French caramel. "I think we have enough potatoes to last today, but we'll need some more tomorrow. Our tortilla supply is getting a little low too. Can you think of anything else I should pick up?" Nancy set the two cups at a small table next to the window. A drop of rain was still on Mary's cheek. But it wasn't rain.

"Mary, what's wrong?" She touched Mary's hand. "Here I've been babbling away without really paying attention--I'm sorry."

"It's all right, I'm fine." Her voice caught, and she took a breath. "Last night John told me he wants a divorce."

"Huh? I thought everything had been going so well for you two."

"So did I. It just came out of the blue."

"But what did he say? Is it an early mid-life crisis? Does he have the hots for a 25-year-old?"

"Well, he didn't really give a reason. He just said he thought it would be best for us."

"<u>Best</u> for you? In what way would that be good for you? Sounds to me like a pretty weak reason."

"Yeah. I suppose."

Nancy took a tentative sip of her coffee, testing to see if it was still too hot to drink. She looked into her friend's eyes. "So what did you say?"

"Um, the funny thing is, I almost felt like I expected this. I didn't really say anything. Maybe I don't have the energy to fight it. But we <u>have</u> been happy together. It just doesn't make any sense."

They sat in silence. Nancy said, "You don't have to work today if you don't feel up to it. I can fill in for you over lunch and call Mark to fill in this afternoon. Just take some time for yourself."

"No, thanks, I think I need to work just to keep my mind off this. I tell myself that I'll go home this afternoon and everything will go back to normal. I tell myself that this is just a bad dream...but part of me accepts it too-- that's the scary part."

Nancy sipped her coffee, trying to think of something to say. She rested her hand lightly on Mary's forearm. "John will come to his senses. He would be crazy to lose you."

They finished their coffee and continued working. To lighten the mood, Nancy put a country station on the radio--a concession to Mary's poor taste in music--and turned up the volume. She took a sharp knife and began to cut potatoes for soup.

Jaime Saldivar made his entrance fifteen minutes before opening. Nancy glanced up to see what he was wearing. Tight black jeans, alligator skin cowboy boots, and a deep blue shirt with pointed collars the length of 747 wings. Pretty conservative.

"It's time to party, ladies," he said. "I'll mix the margaritas if you'll get the chips and salsa." He rummaged in the kitchen cabinets, pretending to look for tequila.

Mary laughed. "What's the occasion, Jaime? You get lucky last night?"

"Not like you think, pervert. In fact, the lovely Sylvia Wilson consented--no, enthusiastically agreed!--to accompany me on a date tonight. It will be an evening of romance that she will never forget...Hey, what's with that?"

He walked to the bucket and stared at the dripping light bulb above it.

"A leak," Nancy said.

Jaime grinned and pulled a piece of paper from under the counter. He scribbled something on it and taped it to the bucket. Nancy put down her knife and walked over to look. "Soup of the day," the sign read.

"Ha ha," Nancy said. Drop by drop, the bucket was filling with gray water.

At 10:00 Nancy plugged in the purple neon "Open" sign, and the mid-morning coffee drinkers started to drift in. They didn't order food, but Nancy didn't begrudge them taking up space. The markup on the coffee was high, especially if they ordered exotic lattes or mochas. In the back of her mind, she knew it was her only hope for eventually running the place in the black.

Jaime cheerfully kept the mugs filled, stopping at the tables to joke with the customers. Nancy helped Mary in the kitchen, occasionally poking her head out the door and greeting people she knew.

The lunch crowd finally arrived, a sodden group of townspeople who filled the place with noise and laughter. Nancy helped Jaime, balancing plates on her arm and drinks on trays. It was her favorite time of the day, the reason she bought the restaurant in the first place.

In mid afternoon she unfolded her umbrella and hunched into the downpour. She crossed Alder Street, stepping wide to avoid the dirty water rushing in the gutter. She took her time, checking out the window displays of boutiques and junk shops. The town was, to put it charitably, a loose collection of organized clutter. It had its own charm, ugly in an endearing way, like a basset hound. A few years ago, the town fathers and mothers had attempted to impose an artificial theme on the buildings, arguing that business would increase only if the property owners would slap on the facade of a cowboy western town. Two enthusiastic boosters complied, to hilarious effect: the locals snickered at the fake building fronts and called the owners "Doc" and "Miss Kitty." The city council and chamber of commerce reluctantly conceded that there was something to be said, after all, for fierce independence, and chaos once again reigned in building design.

Nancy crossed High Street and climbed into a residential area. Fat raindrops smashed into limp flower petals on the rhododendrons in the front yards she passed. The rain beat a drum roll on her umbrella and sizzled on the street pavement.

She crossed her yard on a winding footpath, turning a blind eye to the weeds growing under her azaleas. Unlocking the door, she savored the stillness of the house, a silence that she knew would be shattered in moments. She picked up the phone and called Sarah, her babysitter, letting her know she was home early.

As she started preparing dinner (macaroni and cheese, good dinners having gone by the wayside since she started cooking for a living), the door burst open and the house filled with noise. Her children, along with a handful of friends, streamed in, dropping a wet collection of backpacks and coats on the kitchen floor and table.

"Hi Mom!"

"Hey Maddie, how was school?"

"Fine. I got a A on my science project..." Her voice trailed off with the stampede of Nikes as the horde moved downstairs to the bonus room. Nancy shook her head and went back to grating a block of Velveeta. Outside, a dark cloud moved over the western sky, blocking what remained of the daylight.

***

Later, after the hour-long ritual of getting the four kids to bed, she and Bruce floated in the hot tub. The rain had eased off some, making a soft rattle against the corrugated plastic roof over the tub. The bitter smell of bromide mixed with the cool and moldy scent of the air blowing in from the back yard.

"So how was your day?" he asked. She paused

before answering, wondering how their lives had become so hectic. He had been home for four hours, and this was the first opportunity they had had to talk. Unless you counted the happy babble that had flowed over the dinner table.

"It went fine," she said, then told him about Mary Mowatt, and her husband who thought he wanted a divorce. She still found it hard to accept.

"Things really are getting weird," Bruce said.

"I guess."

"At the bank, too"

"How so?"

"Well, a bunch of our customers apparently emptied their savings accounts over the past week, and today they brought their money back in--in cash."

"Well, at least they brought it back." She listened to the rain for a moment. "Why did they pull out their money in the first place?"

"No idea. One of the tellers asked, and all the customer said was something like they were worried about a financial crisis. That's obviously something that we don't like to talk about, so we didn't pursue it. Kind of like joking about bombs at an airport security gate."

Nancy propped her legs on his knees and leaned back, letting her blond hair float on the water. A gust of wind shook the roof, sending a cascade of rain over the edge. Somewhere under the bushes, a frog added his song to the rhythm of the night.

2

It was at 11:05 the following morning when Isaac Cohen told Nancy about the operation foul-up.

"Did you hear about the latest medical scandal?" he boomed from the café door, shaking a wide brimmed bush hat onto the carpet.

"About what?" Nancy asked. They were running behind in preparing for lunch, and she was in the middle of switching out the CO_2 canister for the soft drinks.

"They almost took out Shirley Collins' kidney!"

Nancy emerged from behind the drink machine, suddenly alert. "Go on," she said.

"Yeah, well, you knew she had her baby, right? So they kept her in for an extra day, something to do with the complicated delivery I guess, and the next thing she knows, they're wheeling her into the operating room. She was with it enough to start asking questions, and managed to convince them that she really didn't need a new kidney before they put her under. She said they got it all straightened out, and she's sure glad to be home."

"But how did it happen?"

"I don't know. I guess her name just showed up on their surgery schedule. Maybe it was a computer glitch." Isaac reached back and shook the rain out of his hair, tied in a thick gray tail.

"So, anyhow, how's the baby?" Nancy asked. "It's

a boy, right?"

"Yeah. I forget what they named him. Nathan, or Jason, or something like that. Hey, I gotta go."

"You're not even going to buy a cup of coffee?"

"Nope. Sorry. Here…" He dug into his pocket and put a quarter on the counter."

"What's that for?"

"Help you pay the rent." He grinned and spun on his heel.   Jaime Saldivar, resplendent in turquoise pants and a pink flowered shirt, opened the door for him. Nancy shook her head and bent to lift a full CO^2 canister.

"So, Jaime, how did the evening go?" Nancy called. "Who was it this time? Sylvia someone?"

"Wilson. Sylvia Wilson," he said, wounded that she didn't remember. "And I'm not sure this is an appropriate topic of discussion between a boss and her employee, especially with young ladies present." He nodded at Mary, who guffawed through the kitchen window.

"Hey, you brought it up. 'An evening of romance that she wouldn't forget,' or something like that. So, was it?"

He winked at her. "You will have to ask Miss Wilson, but I can tell you this: we have another hot date tonight. And I mean very hot. As in caliente. And piquante. Hot hot hot." He did a dance, to the amusement of old Mrs. Koepke, the first of the stream of lunch customers.

In mid afternoon, Nancy carried the cash and checks across the street in a green zippered bag. Bruce had started his banking job here at the Cedar Creek branch, but two years ago he had been offered a promotion as the head of the commercial loan department in a branch 40 minutes away. The bank seemed to take perverse pleasure in forcing people to commute for a living. Few of the staff at the Cedar Creek branch actually lived in Cedar Creek, most of them driving at least 20 miles each way. One of them, a vice president, actually lived within a few blocks of Bruce's branch. It was crazy. Bruce had once calculated that if they could all trade jobs, the staff in just the five Oregon branches of the bank could save 104,000 gallons of gas a year and 52,000 hours of their lives.

On a whim, she sat down at the New Accounts desk before leaving. Polly Harper was an old high school friend.

"Polly," she said, leaning forward, her elbows on the cheap Formica-and-chipboard desk, "has anything odd been happening at this branch?"

"Heck yeah," Polly said.

"Like what?"

"Like Stu Smiley is trying to grow a moustache," she whispered. "It looks like he stepped on a caterpillar and glued what was left of it to his lip." She giggled.

Nancy smiled, and forced herself not to look over her shoulder to see if she could see the young assistant manager. "Anything else?" she asked.

Polly paused for a moment. "Well, there is something, but I don't think I'm supposed to tell you."

"That's OK." Nancy glanced toward the lobby to see if anyone was within earshot. "How about just leaving out names?"

"Hmm. Well, all right." She leaned toward Nancy. "See, we process a lot of the automatic payroll deposits for businesses in Cedar Creek. They just send over the account codes and amounts on a disk, or on-line. Then the payroll amounts get transferred from the business' account to the employees' accounts. Hey, you should look into it for your employees. Or do you already do it that way?"

"No, my payroll computer consists of a sheet of paper and calculator. I guess I'm old-fashioned."

"Well, they didn't catch it for a while. In fact, I'm not sure they ever would have, except McDonalds, uh, the business, was checking their statements. They found an eighteen thousand dollar transfer to one of our customer accounts—and the customer wasn't even an employee of theirs."

"Somebody typed in a wrong code, huh?"

"No, that's the thing. We have to investigate that stuff—part of our quality assurance program, or whatever they call it. The on-line transfer came through the way it was supposed to, with the right accounts, and it generated the right transactions. They even ran the transfer through the computer again, to see what would happen."

"And?"

"Nothing. Everything worked like it should have."

"Hmm." A log truck rolled down the street in front of the bank, rattling the plate glass windows. "I bet your customer was surprised to get the extra money."

"Oh, I don't think he even noticed it. See, it was a money market account, and he keeps a pretty big balance there. At least he didn't report it when we mailed the statements."

"Would you have?"

Polly smiled. "Like getting a card that says, 'Bank error in your favor,' huh? I wonder… But he wasn't upset when Stu called him and said we had to transfer the eighteen grand back out. Just said, 'Yeah, whatever.'"

The phone rang on her desk.

"Go ahead and take it," Nancy said. "I'll see you later."

"Sure. See ya."

***

A half hour later, Nancy stood shoulder to shoulder with a dozen other parents at the back of Mr. Zimmerman's second-grade class at Cedar Creek Grade School. She found herself wondering if the traditional end-of-school party was something that the teachers, parents, and children did because they thought the others enjoyed it, while each privately wished they were doing something else. But the excitement in the children's faces was more than pre-vacation giddiness--they were genuinely proud to show off their ceramic ash trays and reports on the animals of Venezuela. The teachers, for their part, seemed to be thrilled to have an activity where they didn't have to teach basic algebra to boys who stuck pencils in their nostrils and girls who giggled for no apparent reason. Nancy remembered the feeling well. And on the other side of the desk as a proud parent, she really wouldn't have missed it.

Mr. Zimmermann gave the usual speech about how much the students had accomplished and how much he enjoyed teaching them, and introduced the opening act: a puppet show.

A boy named Nick was the voice for one of the puppets. Nancy could hardly hear his soft words from behind the cardboard screen. Stage fright from a young man who no doubt was perfectly capable, in class, of bellowing out such useful information as "Jennifer has a hole in her underwear!" The story was about a bear and a lion who had the integrity to do what was right, rather than to cave in to peer pressure and follow the sheep. A precursor to next year's DARE training, no doubt.

There was a group poetry reading and a demonstration of the class science project, and mercifully the program came to a close. A couple of the kids poured punch and set some bland cookies on plates.

Sam, age seven, took Nancy by the hand and gave her a tour of the classroom, proudly showing her his finger paintings tacked to the wall.

"Look at this one, Mom," he said. "It's my favorite."

"That looks nice," she said, squinting at a blob of blue and green color. "Um, what is it?"

"A fish! Hiding in seaweed. And a rock."

After a while Sam pulled himself free of her hand and joined a group of other boys who were huddled around a snake cage. Nancy found herself standing next to Claudia, one of the boys' mothers.

"They seem so happy and carefree here," Claudia said. "Too bad it isn't always like this at home for them."

"Yeah, some of them do have it rough."

Claudia looked around to make sure no small ears were listening, and said quietly, "Did you hear about Ashley's mom, Karen?"

"No..." said Nancy hesitantly, not sure she wanted to get into any gossip, but immediately curious.

"Well, I hear that she's having an affair with Dave Kendall. And she's not being very discreet about it--even her kids know something is up."

"Oh no, that can't be. They both had solid marriages, last I heard."

"I know. But it's true."

Nancy shook her head. "How can people mess up their lives like that?"

"I know. And always, it seems it's the kids who end up on the short end."

3

Betty Scruggs peered through the bottom of her bifocals, starting a new row on the afghan she was knitting for the church bazaar. She unrolled the ball of blue yarn a few turns, placing it carefully on her lap. The needles moved expertly, pulling and guiding the yarn. She had been doing this so many years the afghan practically knitted itself.

On the TV a CNN reporter was giving a solemn and urgent account of a terrorist bombing somewhere in the Middle East. Betty struggled to catch the words. This isn't news, she thought. It's an old story, centuries old; only the technology has changed. She had gone there herself, twenty years ago after she had retired from teaching. She and Howard had been part of a Holy Land tour the church had put together. The images formed in her mind, of the Jordan River, Jerusalem, Nazareth, and Bethlehem. Howard had insisted on parting from the tour's itinerary, and they took in the modern cities of Tel Aviv and Beirut, with stopovers in Athens and Rome on their way home. The young woman at the consulate in Portland had advised them against Beirut—some kind of skirmishes had been going on at the time—but they had avoided the dangerous parts of the city, and saw instead normal people going about their lives as they had been doing for decades.

The blare of the TV noise stopped for a moment, and Betty dimly heard a whistling sound. She put the yarn and knitting needles on the side stand and worked her way up from the chair. In the kitchen, she slid the teakettle off the burner, then reached into the cupboard for a cup and saucer and a bag of English Breakfast. She could feel the heat from the stove on her forearm, and remembered she hadn't turned the burner off. She twisted the knob, and then poured the boiling water into her cup.

Leaving the tea to steep, she moved to the window and watched a dozen juncos flitting around the bird feeder. Howard had made it--years ago--out of cedar stained dark brown and had hung it on a branch of the huge maple tree in the back yard. Rain was silently dripping off the corners, forming a puddle in the grass below. The juncos seemed unconcerned. A towhee flipped seeds and shells out of the grass on the edge of the puddle.

As Betty was checking her tea, she heard a sound, barely audible above the blare of the TV in the next room. It was the phone. She picked it up, wondering how long it had been ringing.

"Hello?"

"Hello, Betty? This is Shirley Finn. How are you doing?"

"Shirley? Is that you?"

"Yes, Betty. I said, how are you doing?"

"Oh. I'm just working on my knitting. The blue blanket."

"Did you decide to make it full size?"

Betty heard it as "full eyes," and it didn't make any sense. She didn't respond.

"Listen, Betty, the reason I called is that we have a

prayer request. Okay?"

"A prayer request. Yes."

She sat at the desk under the phone and pulled out a small pad of paper and a pen.

"The request is for Sandy Britten. Her father just passed away yesterday. Did you get that?"

Betty quickly scribbled on the pad of paper. "Yes. I will make the calls. Thank you for letting me know."

She turned off the TV and settled herself into her sewing chair, and took four deep breaths to clear her thoughts. Then she prayed.

After a time, she went back to the kitchen and sat at the breakfast table, by the phone. There were eight people on her list. To keep her mind sharp, she had worked on memorizing their phone numbers. She called the first one, Gretchen Benford.

"Hello, Gretchen? I'm calling with a prayer request. It's for Andy Britten. His father just passed away."

***

When she bought it, Nancy had a romantic notion that the restaurant would be a good backdrop to conversation and friendships with the people of the town. She had a teaching degree and had been a second grade teacher for a few years before Maddie, her oldest, was born. Nancy had started to become restless even before the kids were all in school, but she had no desire to resume teaching. She had heard through a friend that Betsy's Tea Shop was closing, and the business would be for sale. Although it took a lot of soul searching and long conversations with Bruce, she knew she had found her new career.

They had to dip into savings that they had set aside for college education to buy the restaurant and equipment; before they were done, their house was pledged as security for a loan. She didn't want to limit herself to a single theme or kind of food; her menu included a few Mexican dishes, fresh caught trout and salmon, exotic burgers, and a variety of salads. The downside of her eclectic taste was the need to install a grill and hood, espresso and latte machines, and a few kegs and taps for local microbrews.

Nancy's first action, though, had been to pull off the frilly curtains and strip the flowered wallpaper. In their place she painted off-white walls that only served as a background for art displays, odds and ends from antique stores, hanging plants, and selected pages from old Far Side calendars. Her interior decorating scheme was artfully arranged clutter, and she felt it gave the place a cozy feel, with plenty to catch the eye while customers waited for their entrees over nachos and beer.

These first steps fulfilled part of her dream of building a business that was hers, that reflected a part of her mind and her soul. The next part--making the restaurant run like the one in her dreams--was much harder. She was shocked to find that it was a struggle just to keep the business in the black. Even when her start-up expenses were behind her, she divided her hours into net revenue and discovered that she was earning less than minimum wage. In the good months.

Nancy sat on a stool in a corner of the kitchen staring at a column of numbers. The smell of hot oil from the deep fat fryer began to fill the room.

"How does it look?" Mary asked. She poured flour

into a bowl, raising a small cloud.

"Not so good. We have too many Safeway bills." It was her own fault—rushing out to buy last minute items instead of stocking up through her wholesale supplier. "I don't know how I'm going to pay them."

"Maybe they'll give us a little extra time."

"Yeah. The payments go to California. They probably handle too many to miss a few from me."

She slid the stack of invoices into a corner of the desk, trying to put them out of her mind. "So, has John come to his senses yet, or is he still being crazy?"

Mary paused from her stirring. "Well, it's strange. He's still sweet to me, like nothing has happened. But he's saying he has to move out. Live with his brother, or something like that. I can't figure out what I've done."

"What <u>you've</u> done? Mary, this isn't your fault. He just needs a good knock on the head. Or counseling. You need to get him to go in and talk to a shrink."

"I've tried. He refuses to go to counseling, and I even offered to go with him. Says it's just something he has to do. He has to 'find himself.'"

"Ugh, what a line. Who came up with that nonsense in the first place?"

Mary shrugged and went back to her mixing, fighting back a tear.

"Listen," Nancy said, "If you need anything, like a place to stay, just let me know, okay?"

Mary nodded silently. Nancy waited a moment, then went out to the main room to help Jaime set the tables.

"Did you see this one?" he asked, nodding toward the far wall.

"No, I can't see anything. I'm blinded by your

shirt." It was canary yellow, contrasting with his black pants and leather zip-up boots.

He chuckled. "It's another leak."

Nancy walked closer to look. A trickle of water wandered down the wall, leaving a dark semi circle in the carpet. Great, another call to the roof repair guy, and another bill to pay.

*****

Mac O'Connor was napping in his Reclina-Rest when the phone rang. It didn't register in his consciousness until the fifth ring. He blinked and sat up with a start, spilling a thick book—Bird Watching in South America—onto the floor. He pulled the lever for the footrest and slowly stood up, steadying himself against the arm of the chair. The telephone continued to ring.

It was only four steps to the desk. Mac considered the distance and launched himself across the floor on stiff legs. He stopped himself with one hand on the desk, and picked up the phone with the other.

"Yes?" he barked.

The voice on the other end sounded distant. It must be old Mrs. Scruggs, from the prayer chain. Who else would be calling him in the middle of the day? He struggled to make out the words. She never spoke loud enough.

When she was finished, he put down the phone and eased himself into the straight-backed desk chair. He pulled open a drawer and dug through a heap of paper, looking for his call list. He believed in the power of prayer, but he wondered how well it worked for complete strangers. He had never heard of this Andy person. Must be someone's relative, probably in some distant part of the country. He would save this one for the collection of people he prayed for when he said grace before his evening meal.

He would cook up some fat man chili, a recipe from his days long ago in the logging camps, back when he was spry enough to jump from trunk to trunk in his corks, hauling the heavy bell end of the choker on its cable. He would pour in a little Snappy Tom, some cheddar cheese, a few splashes of beer. He'd pay the price later in the night, but there was enough to interrupt his sleep anyway, and a little indigestion was worth it. Con carne, of course, but he couldn't remember if he had set out the ground beef to thaw.

He shuffled into the kitchen and squinted at the counter, looking for the block of meat wrapped in white butcher paper. It wasn't there. He opened the freezer door gingerly, bracing himself for an avalanche of bags of meat, frozen peas, half-full ice cream cartons, bread, and assorted leftovers. The stack held, precariously, and he stabbed a hand at a bag of meat, slamming the door shut before anything else could escape. He tossed the brick-hard meat on the counter and tried to remember what he was doing before he came out to the kitchen.

He gave up, and tried retracing his steps. He leaned against the kitchen doorframe and peered at his recliner. A book was on the floor, so he must have been reading. A bird book. And a desk drawer was open. Had he been in the process of looking up some of his own notes?

Aha! The list. He was supposed to call the people on the chain. A chore that would interrupt his day, but it wouldn't get done unless he applied himself to it.

Mac O'Connor sat himself at the desk and dialed the first name on the list. He got her answering machine.

"Stephanie. Mac here. I've got something for the prayer chain." He paused to try to remember the name. His memory wasn't what it was twenty years ago when he was a youthful seventy, but it still wasn't bad. That was it! He had heard it as Andy Brennan, but she must have been calling about Andy Brandon, the new manager of the Cedar Creek Inn. "Andy Brandon. Andy Brandon's father passed. Okay."

***

Mid morning a tall older man burst in, shaking his hat onto the floor.

"Hey Isaac, what's new?" Nancy said.

"Not much. I just had to get out of the studio for a while. How's your mocha today?"

"As good as ever. I'll make you a tall one."

Nancy slid a mug under the tap of the espresso machine. Isaac called out, "Guess what? The Hartsmith Gallery said they wanted to run an exhibit of my water colors!"

"Isaac! That's super! When will it be?"

"Next month, from the third through the seventeenth."

"Well, I hope they don't sell them all. I keep hoping you'll give me your painting of Horsetail Falls. Just call it a gift to charity. See, I've got the perfect place for it right there..."

"Sure, right under the restroom sign. Not the kind of image that goes with a world class artist like me, ha ha."

Isaac's brown eyes glinted. "But O.K., I promise, if no one buys the painting for my grossly inflated price of $75, I'll give it to you. That should be worth free coffee for ten years, or a hundred free marguerites...let's see, that would come out to a whole ounce of tequila the way you water them down."

"Very funny."

While Nancy was adding chocolate to the coffee, a woman came into the cafe, wiped the rain off her glasses, and joined Isaac at the counter. She put her rain hat on the stool next to her and shook out her blond curls.

Isaac said, "So how're you doing, Katharine?"

"Just fine. What are we drinking, anyhow?"

"Strong Irish coffee."

"Works for me."

After a minute, Nancy slid the mugs in front of them and winked at Isaac. Katharine took a careful sip, sucking in air to cool it. "Funny, tastes more like mocha to me."

"Sorry to let you down. Well, how did Joshua's graduation go?"

Katharine described her son's high school graduation ceremony and the emotions that went with it. The conversation shifted to the end of school in general and Nancy mentioned Sam's class party.

"You know, I shouldn't spread rumors, but one of the moms told me something that's been bugging me. She said that Karen Smith—do you know her?—is having an affair."

"Hmm. Plenty of that going around," Katharine said.

"Yeah," Nancy said. "But she is such a good mother—always putting on creative parties for her kids, and volunteering in their classrooms. And she and her husband do such fun stuff. Did you know a couple of months ago they climbed Mt. Adams together?"

"I thought you said fun stuff. No wonder she's playing the field," Isaac said.

"I'm not sure I know her," Katharine said. "And who's the guy?"

"Dave Kendall, from what I hear," Nancy said.

Katharine shook her head. "I don't think I know him either."

Nancy hoisted herself onto the stool on her side of the counter. "I don't know what's going on. Another one of my friends is having marital problems, and it just came out of the blue."

Katharine sipped her mocha. "Yes, I know what you mean. There's a couple in our church that are going through some difficult times, too."

"Who?" Isaac asked. "Inquiring minds want to know."

Katharine hesitated. "Well...it's pretty much common knowledge, so I guess it's okay to say. It's Sharon and Dave Randall."

"Nope, don't know them," Isaac said. "The names sound familiar, though."

"I thought you knew everybody in this little town," Katharine said. "By the way, I don't want to complain, but this weather is driving me batty. See if you can do something about it, will you Nancy?"

"Yeah, I'll get right on it."

"Actually, I'm surprised the City Council hasn't formed a committee for it. They have committees on the economy, on youth crime, on community values, and a bunch of other stuff they can do absolutely nothing about.

They might as well add weather to the list."

Something was nagging at Nancy's thoughts. "Maybe they sound familiar because they sound the same," she said slowly.

"Huh?" Isaac said.

"The names. You said that Sharon and Dave Randall sound familiar. Maybe that's because their names <u>sound</u> like Karen and Dave Kendall."

"Could be." Isaac shrugged.

"Mmm. Interesting," Katharine said. "Did you notice the weather guy on channel 7 keeps coming up with different ways to say 'wet'? He started with words in English but now he's having to resort to French and German and Japanese and who knows what other languages. This morning he said moo yay or something like that. I guess it's the only way he can make the forecast different every day."

"I usually watch channel 9," Isaac said.

Nancy finished her mocha, letting her eyes follow the beads of water as they collected and slid down the front windows of the restaurant. "I better get back to work," she said.

***

Stephanie Ong carried her groceries in and set them on the counter. The red light was flashing on her answering machine, and she pushed the play button. The first message was from her boss at the Far East Portland Oriental Food Market, reminding her that she needed to come in an hour early the next morning to help take inventory. The second was from Mac O'Connor. She listened to the prayer request and started to call the people on her list, then realized that she needed to put some of the groceries away. Especially the frozen dumplings.

She heard the front door open. "Hi Sabrina. How was school?"

"Fine," her sixteen-year-old daughter yelled. "The band teacher moved me up to second trumpet but then…" Her voice faded out as she went upstairs to her bedroom. Stephanie glanced at her call list, and decided that it would be better to wait until after dinner, anyway. More people would be home then.

***

Dinner for Nancy Mackay that night consisted of take-out pizza and salad. Her restaurant customers were eating better than her family was, but if Bruce was upset about it, he didn't complain. Besides, they both had jobs, so if he wanted a home-cooked meal, he could always cook it himself. The kids, for their part, wolfed down the pizza, cheeks and elbows smeared with cheese and tomato sauce.

"I got a call from Lorene at the Cedar Creek branch today," Bruce said as they cleared the table. "She said we were overdrawn on our business account."

Nancy paused, holding the empty pizza box carefully so the crumbs wouldn't spill. "Oh? I wonder why she called you instead of me."

"She said it's the third time it's happened in the past two months, and the bank is getting concerned."

She folded and stuffed the box into the garbage can under the sink. "They shouldn't worry. I'm making every loan payment."

"On time?"

"Mostly."

Bruce paused for a moment. "Is the restaurant going to make it? Lorene said it was the loan payment that put the account in the hole."

Nancy was going to blurt out something sharp in defense, but caught herself. He had asked if <u>the restaurant</u> was going to make it, being careful not to put the blame on her. "I think so. Every week the receipts go up a little bit. We're starting to get a good crowd for lunch. I want to put some coupons in the paper, too, but that would cost more money. And I've had to call the roof repair guy twice, and the tourists just aren't showing up. It seems every time I get a few dollars ahead, something breaks or a supplier raises his price." Her voice caught.

He had his back to her, emptying plates from the dishwasher. "Well, keep an eye on the account balance. We can move a few dollars from the money market account if we have to."

***

Stephanie Ong sat with her husband, drinking tea. Sabrina had left the dinner table in a snit, upset because her parents made her finish her homework instead of going over to Rachel's house to watch a movie. The house was quiet until the phone rang. Her husband answered it, frowned, said "no" a couple of times, and hung up. "Some kind person is concerned that we have a crack in our windshield," he said, and chuckled.

The phone call reminded Stephanie that she had some calls to make herself. The list was still on the counter. She called the first person.

"Hello Roy. This is Stephanie Ong."

Before Stephanie could relay the message, Roy told her he had been meaning to call, to ask her if she could lead his junior high Sunday school class next week. She agreed, and they discussed the lesson plan.

"Oh, and Roy, I have a message for the prayer chain. We are asked to pray for Andy Brandon." She stopped to remember what the message was. "I believe he is passing a kidney stone. Something like that."

***

Nancy's day started bad and got worse. She took her car to work, partly because she had some errands to run, and mostly because she was sick of the rain. When she pulled out of her driveway, the steering felt mushy and the car pulled to the right. After a hundred feet, she could no longer ignore the rumbling sound, and pulled over to the curb. She sighed and put the car in park and found that, in fact, the right front tire was as flat as Kansas. Bruce was long since gone, and the kids had already been swept up by the school bus—not that they would be much use changing a tire—so she was left with the job herself.

After some searching, she found the jack in the engine compartment. The wingnut that held it on its post was covered with grit and oil, and she needed to use both hands to get it loose. It barely fit under the car, and she had to stand in the gutter to give herself enough clearance to wind it up with the cheap stamped metal lug wrench. The drizzle collected in her hair and started to drip down her back. She could feel the dampness seep through the seams of her shoes. It took forever to turn the jack high enough.

Then the lug nuts wouldn't budge. She lifted until her back burned and the car swayed on the jack, but the wrench wouldn't move. She remembered then that when Bruce did it, he stomped down on the wrench <u>before</u> the car was up on the jack, enough to start the nuts turning, then he lifted the car.

She stared at the flat tire, feeling the rain make its way through her coat, and gave the wrench a kick. The car wobbled precariously and the nut didn't move. She muttered a curse and lowered the jack. When the car was finally resting on the rubber again, she positioned the wrench and hopped up on one foot. Her first jump missed and her foot slammed into the gutter puddle, jarring her leg and soaking her pants. She looked over the shoulder to see if any of the neighbors were watching, ready to feel torn between embarrassment and anger that they hadn't come out to help. No faces peered from the windows, at least as far as she could see.

Another more carefully planted kick, and the first nut groaned loose. She got the other five started, and bent down to wind up the jack once more. Some of the wet road grime rubbed onto her coat when she hefted the flat into the trunk.

When she got the job done, Nancy wiped her hands on a rag that she found under the back seat, and thought about backing the car into her driveway to clean up and change clothes. But she was late enough as it was, so she shoved the gear into drive.

She hurried to get the restaurant chores done. Her supplies run after lunch would take her into Portland and she didn't want to go the distance on a doughnut spare that had seemed half flat itself. So mid-morning she took the car to the Les Schwab tire store at the edge of town and ate slightly stale popcorn while they plugged the leak and put the tire back on. Not much tread on it, you really need a new set, a young man with a blond crew cut had said. Not now, not today, Nancy had muttered.

Things finally started looking up as the first lunch customers started trickling in. Her socks had dried, Jaime had remained cheerful in spite of her sour mood, and the place began to fill with conversation and laughter. She put a Rickie Lee Jones CD in the sound system and took orders for black coffee, skinny latte, Moose Drool Ale, and Obsidian Stout. She greeted the customers by name, at least the ones she could remember. Phil Moore, the city manager, came in alone, carrying a soggy copy of the Wall Street Journal. A couple of retirees, Warren and Merle (she didn't know their last names) took their customary booth at the corner. A woman—who had a familiar face and a name that eluded Nancy—sat at one of the small round tables with Andy Brandon who worked at the town's only motel.

She was behind the counter, counting change for one of the early coffee-only customers when she sensed something was wrong. She scanned the room. One of the diners was bent over double, his head nearly in his soup bowl, clutching his side. The woman sitting across from him had leaned forward, her eyes wide in concerned panic. Nancy quickly thanked her customer and moved around the counter.

"Andy, are you all right?" she asked.

"Yeah," he grunted, straightening up slowly. "I don't know what it was. Felt like someone stuck a knife in my side. But now it's gone." He took a deep breath. "Guess I should have held off on the Tabasco with my hash browns this morning, huh?"

His companion laughed in relief.

"Can I get you anything?" Nancy asked.

"No, we're fine," he said.

Phil, the city manager, had lowered his newspaper and narrowed his eyes to see what the commotion was. He pushed his reading glasses on his nose and returned to his paper.

Nancy did a quick tour through the room with a full coffee pot, watching Andy Brandon out of the corner of her eye. He had resumed sipping his soup and talking. Jaime carried out a tray of bacon burgers, holding them above his head like an Italian waiter. Two men—the owner and the sales manager for the Blue Steel metal fabricating shop—walked in, shaking their umbrellas on the entryway carpet. Nancy greeted them, and they took a booth at the side of the room.

She was putting the coffee pot back on the burner when she heard a chair clatter to the floor. Andy Brandon's lunch companion had jumped back, away from the table. Andy himself must have been oblivious to that. He was busy throwing up into his soup bowl.

Conversation in the restaurant stopped. Phil Moore slid a phone out of his coat pocket and quickly dialed a number. Andy's companion stayed a few feet from the table, a stricken look on her face. Andy's eyes were closed and beads of perspiration formed on his forehead. He reached for his napkin and wiped his mouth. Nancy touched his shoulder.

"Is there anything I can do?" she asked quietly.

"No. Sorry," he mumbled. "The pain was incredible. I've never had anything like it." Another wave hit him, and he doubled over, groaning.

Merle, one of the retirees, snatched up his bill and

quietly moved up to the counter. Nancy hesitated, feeling she didn't want to leave Andy alone, but not wanting to stay there either. Jaime said he would take care of it, and rang up the total.

The silence continued. The two men from the Blue Steel shop slipped out the front door, leaving their menus open at their booth. The two retirees quickly left. Phil Moore moved to the front and Nancy thought, what, are they all leaving me here alone? But he just stood at the window, watching calmly.

A siren broke the silence. A rescue rig came to a stop on the highway in front, double-parked in the right lane. Its flashing red lights cut through the drizzle. A pair of paramedics hustled in, and Phil bent to talk to the one in front.

"How are ya doin' buddy?" the paramedic asked. The name "Armstrong" was written on the back of his coat in black letters.

"I'm okay," Andy muttered.

"No he isn't," his companion said.

"Are you his wife?"

"No," she said, looking flustered. "I just work at the motel, too."

"All right. What are the symptoms?"

"Sharp pain," Andy said. "Thought it was gas or something, but it's in the wrong place."

"Does it come and go?"

"Yeah." Andy grimaced and closed his eyes as another wave hit him.

"Sort of down at your side, huh?"

"Yeah," he gasped.

Armstrong looked at his partner, who nodded.

"Sounds like a kidney stone. It isn't life

threatening, so we're not going to transport you, but I want to go to the urgent care clinic."

"Okay." Andy pushed a hand to his side.

"I mean right now."

"Come on, I'll drive you," Andy's employee said. She took him by the elbow, and he got up, shakily. Halfway to the door, she stopped. "Oh, I—"

"Don't worry, I'll cover the bill," Nancy said.

"Hey, thanks."

The paramedics followed them out. A few onlookers had gathered on the sidewalk—the "uh oh squad," as Bruce called them—watching through the window, but they began to disperse. Phil Moore paid Jaime for his meal, and on the way out told Nancy he was sorry for the commotion. It wasn't your fault, she told him, and thanked him for calling the fire department.

It was twelve-fifteen and the restaurant was empty. She looked at the mess on the table, and fell into a chair, feeling her eyes well with tears. Of all the rotten luck. She had hoped to get enough cash in the till to cover her supplies run, but now it would be nearly empty. And having a customer puke on his place setting just wasn't very good advertising. The numbers would probably be down for at least a week.

Jaime swept up a tray, and with his hand wrapped in a napkin, carefully picked up the full soup bowl. Mercifully, he didn't comment.

Nancy did it for him.

"Chunky beef," she muttered.

A snicker erupted from Jaime, then a full laugh. "Good one, Nancy! Chunky beef!"

Mary, watching from the kitchen window, burst out laughing too, and Nancy felt herself start to giggle.

Mary came out and took the tablecloth by the corners. She lifted the whole mess off the table. "Maybe we should re-name the place: the Up-Chuck Wagon. A good cowboy name!" She disappeared into the kitchen, laughing at her own joke.

Nancy shook her head and started clearing the tables. At least she had good staff, not that she was going to be able to pay them on time this month.

***

Isaac Cohen and Katharine Regan burst through the door just before one.

"Hey, where is everyone?" Isaac asked.

"They didn't like our special. Chunky beef soup," Jaime said as he sat at the counter, reading the newspaper.

"Huh?"

"It's a long story," Nancy said, and sat down with them. She told them that a customer had gotten sick and the restaurant had emptied out. Just hasn't been my day, she said, and mentioned the flat tire and how she got soaked on the way in to work.

"Hold on, before you get too far with your sad stories, I need some food," Isaac said.

"Yeah, me too. How about a French Dip and a diet Pepsi?"

"Umm, sounds good," he said. "But just give me a tuna melt on dark rye and a beer."

"Beer? Aren't you working?" Katharine said.

"I work for myself, woman. Who are you, my mother?"

Katharine laughed, and Nancy got up to relay the order to Mary, who had already turned down the burners under the grill.

Nancy returned with the drinks and poured herself an iced tea from a pitcher in the small refrigerator under the counter.

"So who was he?" Isaac said.

"Who was who?" Nancy asked.

"The customer. You know, the one who got sick?"

"Oh. It was Andy Brandon, the motel manager."

Katharine gave her a sharp look. "Was it a kidney stone?"

"Yes," Nancy said. "At least that's what the paramedics thought. But I never knew they caused someone to toss their cookies. How did you guess?"

"I didn't know that either. It's just that I had a message from our church prayer chain last night. Told us to pray for Andy Brandon who was passing a kidney stone."

"Guess it didn't work," Isaac said.

Katharine shrugged.

***

Later that afternoon, when she was stuck in traffic on the way back from Portland, Nancy puzzled over it. How could Katherine's prayer chain have known about the kidney stone <u>before</u> it hit? When she got back to the café, she called the Cedar Creek Inn. A woman answered.

"Hi, this is Nancy Mackay. Andy Brandon isn't in, is he?"

"No, sorry, he's unavailable. Uh, you're the owner of the Fir Away, aren't you?"

"Yes. Were you the one who was with him at lunch?"

"Yeah, tough break for him, huh?"

"How's he doing?"

"Okay, as far as I know. The doctor put him on some pain medication. I didn't hang around at the clinic too long. I guess he just has to ride it out."

"Do you know if he ever had one of those before?"

"A kidney stone? No, I don't think so. He didn't have a clue what hit him."

"And he didn't have any symptoms earlier?"

"No, I think it started when we headed out for lunch. Why?"

"Oh, I just feel bad for him. Tell him I'm sorry he's had to go through that."

"Sure."

She put down the phone and thought about it. Katharine <u>had</u> said the prayer chain call came last night, hadn't she? It didn't make sense. Nancy looked out at traffic driving past the window, windshield wipers sweeping out semi-circles on the car windows and rooster tails of water spraying off the back tires. She shivered and pulled on her coat.

4

Nancy woke up slowly. She heard the sound of pebbles grinding against each other as the waves swept the beach. The children were busy making a sand castle, conferring over design and singing to themselves. A light breeze carried the smell of smoke from a driftwood campfire and flapped an edge of her beach umbrella.

Except that she wasn't at the beach. She opened an eye. The sound of pebbles must have been one of the kids—probably Jake—pawing through the bucket of Legos, building some sort of space exploration contraption. She slid a foot over to Bruce's side of the bed. He was already up, frying bacon as part of his weekend breakfast ritual. She could hear the raucous sound of cartoons on a distant TV and the thumping of water dropping down the downspout outside her window. She stared at the ceiling and pulled the covers to her chin.

She had a weekend cook, Ernesto Ortiz, who moonlighted from his job at the Mountain Peaks Country Club, and Jaime worked Saturday, so she didn't have to go in. But it was still hard to ignore the business. Ernesto was actually a better cook than Mary, and resourceful too, so there was probably nothing to worry about. As long as they had enough customers. Had she remembered to put the coupon in this week's issue of the paper?

She squeezed her eyes shut, forcing herself to

think of something else. She tried to transport herself to the beach scene in her waking dream, but now it was drizzling there and the ocean seemed cold. A hot shower would fix that.

At breakfast a happy chatter floated over the table. Sam's hair stuck out wildly. Maddie carefully filled each square of her waffle with syrup. Indigo swung her feet as she nibbled on her bacon, the ears on her bunny slippers flapping as they hit the end of each trajectory. Jake took a break from eating to poke sticky fingers at his space vehicle.

"So. What do you guys want to do today?" Bruce asked.

"Let's play soccer," Sam said. "I can get Justin and some other--"

"No, let's go to OMSI," Indigo said.

Maddie grunted in disgust. "Too crowded."

"Yeah, OMSI," Jake said. "I want to go in the submarine again."

"Hey, don't they have a bungee jumping thing showing on the—what do you call it?"

"Omnimax?" Bruce said.

"Uh huh," Sam said. "That would be sweet."

"What do you think, Nancy?"

Six tickets to the museum of science and industry would be expensive. But Bruce still had a decent job, and they could afford it.

"Sure," she said.

"I want to stay home and play with Rachel" Maddie said.

Bruce flipped the paper open to the comic pages. "Come along, big girl. You'll have a good time. Besides, we'll get home in plenty of time for you to play."

She groaned and got up from the table.

"Put your plate in the dishwasher," Bruce said.

He and Nancy cleaned up the kitchen as the children got dressed.

"I really should be staying home to mow the lawn," Bruce said. "It's starting to look like a hay field."

"What, and leave me with a carload of munchkins? Besides, the grass is too wet to mow."

"Yeah, I guess. I just want to do something outdoors for a change."

Nancy stared vacantly out the car window as it hurtled down the highway toward Portland. Bruce drove and listened to Car Talk on the radio. Indigo was between them on the bench seat, holding a doll and calmly watching the traffic. Something seemed out of place—a strange sort of glow, as if a stage light had suddenly been turned on. Nancy leaned forward and looked up.

"I'll be darned," she said.

"What, Mom?" Indigo asked.

"It's the sun. It's poking through a hole in the clouds."

Indigo looked at her, curious.

"Yes, I know," Nancy said. "I've seen the sun before. It's just been a while."

A mile farther down the road they hit a light drizzle. Bruce turned the wipers on.

Inside the Oregon Museum of Science and Industry, Maddie and the boys took off for the Turbine Hall. Bruce followed at a distance, looking at the exhibits and keeping an eye on them.

"Come on Mom, I want to see the snake," Indigo said, and pulled Nancy's hand.

The two of them made their way upstairs and

stood in front of Bubba, a 13-foot python. The huge snake was sleeping. Indigo got close, but made no attempt to wake the reptile. She took Nancy's hand. "Come on."

She pulled her mother toward a cage. A large white rat with a pink tail ran on an exercise wheel. Another rat, a mottled gray and brown color, stood on a green plastic tower and sniffed the air. Indigo waved at it. The rat jumped down, but Indigo continued to wave.

"I don't think it can see you now," Nancy said.

Indigo gave her an odd look. "You mean the rat?"

"Yes."

"I'm waving at Christine. Why would I wave at a rat?"

"Huh?"

"In case she's watching. It's the RatCam, Mom. Don't you know?"

Nancy bent and looked through the cage. On the far side was a small fisheye lens, with a cable leading to a computer. "Well, I'll be."

She looked at Indigo. How could a five-year-old have figured out that if she stood in a particular spot, she would be broadcast over the Internet? How had she discovered the RatCam in the first place?

As if reading her mind, Indigo said, "We watch it sometimes at Trudy's house. One time, while we were watching, Squeaky Harris walked by and we saw him. He didn't know we were watching. Good thing he didn't pick his nose or something, huh?"

Trudy's mother Sarah watched the kids when they got out of school. Nancy hadn't realized she let the children surf the Net, but she shouldn't have been surprised. "What else do you watch?" she asked.

"We watch the weather at the coast, and in the

mountains. There's a skate park and we watch that sometimes, but I don't know where it is. We play hearts sometimes too, with other people on the Internet."

"Hearts? You know how to play that?"

"Sure. But I don't win much. People always give me the queen of spades. That messes me up."

Nancy squatted down and hugged Indigo's shoulder. "Hi Christine. Can you see us?" She waved at the camera. Indigo giggled.

***

After the trip to OMSI, Nancy and Bruce took a walk, checking on the restaurant and smelling the blooms that were just beginning to emerge on rose bushes. The drizzle was light enough that they didn't bother with an umbrella. She did some paperwork in the evening as Bruce and the kids watched a video. They had a lazy Sunday morning, drinking coffee and reading the paper. They played games with a house full of children—their own and friends from the neighborhood, and walked to the grade school field for a wet game of soccer.

Monday came too quickly. The weekend crew had done a good job cleaning up the kitchen, but the supplies were running low again. It was Jaime's day off, and Sally Dupree, a stay-at-home mom, took his place.

"Where's Mary?" Sally asked after they had finished the normal small talk.

Nancy looked at the antique clock on the west wall. "I don't know. She should have been here by now."

A half hour later Nancy called Mary's home and got no answer. She started to panic. She could get the soup started and handle most of the cooking chores, but that would leave Sally alone in the front. She called Ernesto, the weekend cook, but his wife simply said, "He no here." He must have been working his regular golf club job. She went through the short list of weekend and part time waiters and waitresses, but none of them were home either.

It didn't matter much. There was a trickle of mid-morning coffee customers, but the lunch crowd never materialized. Mondays were usually pretty good, since a few of the other restaurants in town were closed then. This day was different. Maybe seeing a rescue rig parked outside the café last Friday had turned some customers away. Maybe it was just bad luck. By twelve-thirty she had only sold two bowls of soup, a tuna melt, a hamburger, a BLT, and a couple of salads.

The phone rang while Nancy was preparing one of the salads. "Could you get that?" she called out to Sally.

"It's for you," Sally said. "It's John Mowatt."

Nancy slid the salad onto the counter of the pass-through window, wiped her hands on her apron, and took the phone. "John! Where's Mary? I called but no one was at home."

"Yeah. That's what I'm calling about. Sorry it wasn't sooner, but…there wasn't time." His voice was flat and lifeless.

"Is something wrong?"

"She tried to kill herself. Took a bottle of pills."

"Oh no! How is she?"

"The doctor thinks she's going to be okay. But she's pretty out of it now."

"How did you, uh…"

"I started for work and realized I left my wallet at home. When I went to get it, I found her."

"Where is she now?"

"Good Sam Hospital."

Sally hovered nearby, sensing that something was wrong. There were only a few customers in the café.

"I'll come out as soon as I can," Nancy said. She tried to think of some comforting words, but couldn't. "Thanks for calling."

"Sure."

She quietly repeated the conversation to Sally, who was shocked at the news.

"Why would she try to commit suicide?" Sally asked. "Had she been depressed or something?"

"I don't know. Maybe something happened over the weekend," Nancy said, deciding not to go into the details of Mary's marital strife.

Nancy had three more orders to prepare, and busied herself in the kitchen. With so few customers, their net profit for the day wouldn't cover Sally's pay. But she was able to keep up with the cooking, timing it so the hot parts of each meal were finished at the same time so that Sally could deliver them to the table together. She wondered how Mary kept up with it on busy days.

***

The first two of Nancy's children had been born at the old Bess Kaiser hospital. The last two were at Kaiser Sunnyside. All hospitals were the same, and they all brought back memories—none of them good. The pain of childbirth and recovering from a C-Section. Waiting anxiously while Sam's broken leg was x-rayed. Hours spent in her mother's room as she suffered and died from a rapidly spreading cancer.

She pulled into the parking lot of the Good Samaritan Hospital and drove through a few aisles before finding an empty parking space. At the entrance, an old man with several days' stubble sat under a couple of blankets in a wheelchair, sneaking a smoke. Once she got inside, Nancy tried not to breathe the air, knowing it was thick with sickness.

Mary's room was on the fourth floor. Nancy passed the nurses' station and a dozen rooms full of disease and despair. The door was open, and she peered around the corner, almost hoping that the room was empty. John was sitting on a chair with his feet propped on the side of the bed, reading a magazine.

"Hello?" Nancy said.

He looked up and blinked.

"Oh. Hi Nancy." He put his feet down but did not rise. "Come on in."

Mary seemed to be asleep. An IV tube was taped to her arm and her face was a chalky white. There were dark circles under her eyes. Nancy looked away.

"She's been sleeping most of the time," John said.

Nancy muttered a reply, wanting desperately to get out of the hospital. She took the only other chair in the small room and forced herself to look back at Mary.

"What did she take?" she asked, mostly to fill the silence.

"Tylenol. A whole bottle."

"More than the recommended dosage, huh?"

"Yeah."

In the corridor outside, a couple of nurses pushed a gurney and chattered about a movie. One of the wheels had a flat spot and thumped in rhythm with their footsteps. The sounds faded slowly, replaced by conversations in the adjoining rooms. Someone had a television on, tuned to a game show.

A combination of smells, bitter and antiseptic, reminded Nancy that she was still breathing the air.

"Well," she said.

John rolled his magazine into a tube and tapped it on his knee. "It's my fault," he said.

Nancy looked at him. His hair was dark and cut short. His neck bulged over the collar of his Seahawks tee shirt, and his belt buckle was buried under a roll of gut. He had a perpetual five o'clock shadow, and his lower teeth were crooked. Mary was plump and plain-looking herself, and had always spoken of her husband as if he were a dashing young prince. He had built their house with his own hands when he wasn't driving his delivery truck, and served Mary breakfast in bed on Saturday mornings.

"Don't blame yourself," she said.

He shrugged. "You knew about the troubles we was having, right?"

"Yes. Mary mentioned something about it. But it isn't my business."

"Still."

He stood to look out the window. There wasn't much of a view—just another wing of the hospital. Mary stirred and tried to roll over, tangling her arm in the IV tube. Nancy got up, but John moved quicker.

"Here, I can fix it," he said, and gently pulled Mary's arm free. Nancy sat back down.

He leaned against the window sill and crossed his thick arms. "I wish I could take it all back. If she'd gone and died, I don't know what I'd do. Probably just follow her, I guess."

"But if you feel that way…"

"Yeah. I know. Fact is, I really don't know what come over me. I really don't. Like I say, it's all my fault."

"So there's no one else?"

"Heck no. There ain't nobody but her would have me."

Nancy put her chin in her hands and stared at the floor.

"This probably sounds weird, or like some kind of cop out," he said, "but I just woke up one morning feeling like a prisoner and I had to get out. Like I say, I don't know what come over me. The feeling was sure strong, though."

"You say 'was.' Is that, uh, feeling gone now?"

"I guess. Pretty much anyway. It makes no sense."

"But why didn't you agree to counseling when Mary suggested it."

He gave her a quick glance, and Nancy looked down again. It really wasn't her business.

"She told you that, huh?"

"Yes."

"Well, I don't know. Maybe I didn't want to find out I was going bonkers. I didn't want to have to deal with no shrink. I was set to move out, and didn't want nobody to change my mind."

A nurse stuck his head in the doorway. "How are we doing here?" he asked.

"Fine," John said. "She's sleeping."

The nurse took a reading off some kind of monitoring device that was bolted to the wall, and made a note on a chart that was clipped to the foot of the bed.

"We'll see if we can get her to eat something when she wakes up, okay?" the nurse said, and left the room.

Nancy looked at her watch. The kids would be leaving Sarah's house in an hour.

"So have you?" she asked.

"Come again?" John said.

"Have you changed your mind? About moving out?"

"Oh. Sure."

Nancy stood up and touched Mary's rounded shoulder. "I've got to go," she said to John.

"I'll tell her you came."

"Take care of her, okay?"

At the hospital entrance the grizzled smoker was still in his wheelchair. A light mist turned to drizzle and Nancy walked slowly with her chin up, letting the rain rinse away the germs and infection that followed her in an invisible plume.

Before she started the car, she called Sally at the café to get the phone number for the antique store where Katharine worked. Katharine was there.

"Listen, I need to ask you something," Nancy said. "Yes?"

"In that prayer thing at your church, did anyone ask you to pray for Mary Mowatt?"

"You mean the prayer chain? No, not that I remember. Why?"

"How about her husband, John?"

She paused. "No, I don't think so. Like, do you mean recently?"

"Yeah. About ten days ago."

"No, I'm pretty sure."

"Do you write down who you pray for?"

"Sometimes, if I don't know the person. But I just

write it on a scrap of paper when I get the phone message. I don't keep it, if that's what you're wondering. Why are you asking—is something wrong?"

"Well, it's a long story. I'll fill you in when I see you."

Nancy could hear the jingle on the bell tied to the door handle of the antique shop. Katharine's voice, distant, asked if she could help the customer that had apparently entered. There was a pause, then she was back on the line.

"You know, I think there might have been a John somebody around two weeks ago. He might have been in with a list of other people who needed prayer requests."

"Could it have been John Mowatt?"

"No, I think I would have remembered that. His name was different—Moen, or Mullins, something like that."

Nancy was both disappointed and relieved. "Well, thanks. I'll let you get back to your customers."

"Sure, no problem."

A rain drop slid down the windshield. The inside of the glass was getting fogged over.

"Oh, Katharine?"

"Yeah?"

"Just out of curiosity, what were you praying for, when you were praying for that John person? If you can tell me."

"Sure. He had walked out on his wife."

5

The Columbia Temporary Agency was able to supply a cook. Nancy spent an hour with him, going over the menu, how they handled orders, where the spices and measuring containers were kept, how long it took for the gas flames to heat the inch-thick steel griddle. His name was An Phat, and he didn't volunteer much personal information about himself, except that he lived in southeast Portland and had once owned a restaurant himself, in Vietnam.

Nancy called Jaime to see if he could come in early. He readily agreed, but when he arrived, he protested that it had been a sacrifice, in view of his late night dancing and carousing with a blonde named Tiffany. An Phat raised his eyebrows at Jaime's blue satin pants and purple shirt, but said nothing.

She knew Jaime would ask where Mary was, and she had an answer ready. She simply said that Mary wasn't feeling well—the truth, if not the whole truth— and Jaime seemed to accept it. She gave him her cell phone number and told him to call if he or the cook needed anything. Then she set out in the lightly falling rain.

***

Eighty years earlier, the Discovered Treasures shop had been a home. The steep roof had been replaced several times, but the current version was at least fifteen years old and moss clung to the lower edges of the shingles. The original wood siding survived, thin horizontal strips of fir, the edges made round by a dozen coats of white paint. Narrow double-hung windows filled the front of the building, displaying lamps, chests of drawers, a dining table set made of cherry, a plain grandfather clock and a couple of Regulators, a coat rack, and a Rembrandt print in a gilded frame.

The bell jingled as Nancy pushed open the door. The owner, Marge Hofenbaugh, sat behind a stack of papers at an old oak table. She peered up over half glasses.

"Well, it's Nancy Mackay! We don't often have the pleasure of your visits at this time of day anymore."

"Yeah. You know how it goes..." She had spent hours in the shop when she was getting ready to open the Fir Away Café, searching the crowded shelves for knick-knacks and cast off junk. "How's business going?"

"Okay, I suppose. We could use a few more tourists."

"Yeah. I know."

"So can I help you find anything?"

"Well, I'm looking for Katharine, actually."

"Sorry, she's not for sale!" Marge bellowed at her own joke, and took off her glasses to wipe them with her sleeve. "She's in the sorting room, going through some things we got at an estate sale. Go on back."

Nancy passed through shelves stacked with old coffee grinders, waffle makers, egg beaters, irons with fat cloth-covered cords, crock pots and electric skillets. The air held a mixture of smells: dust, a hint of mold, the lemon scent of furniture polish, the electric smell of old motors and wire.

Katharine sat on a swiveling stool, and was bending down to pull something out of a box. Her hair cascaded down, blond waves obscuring her face. An array of white glass bowls and pitchers sat on a cart next to her.

"Hey," Nancy said.

Katharine straightened up and pushed her hair over her shoulders. She grinned. "What are you doing sneaking up on me like that?"

"Marge told me to make sure you were working."

She chuckled. "Why don't you do this for a while, and I'll go run the café."

"Okay. What _are_ you doing, anyway?" Nancy pulled over an oak chair and sat on it.

"We've got to price all this stuff before we put it out for sale. It gets pretty tedious."

"So how do you know what price to put on it?"

"I just guess. And try to remember what people have paid before. Like, what do you think this is worth?"

She handed Nancy a milk glass bowl. The surface was cold to the touch. She ran her fingers over the bumps on the outside surface, and hefted it to get a sense of the weight.

"Oh, I don't know. Twenty cents?"

Katharine laughed. "Would you believe five bucks?"

"Yeah? Shows what I know."

"They don't make much of this anymore."

Nancy looked at the cart full of milk glass bowls. "I think I know why."

Katherine laughed and bent to pick up another bowl. She stuck an adhesive label on the bottom and wrote a price with a felt pen.

"Marge trusts you with these management decisions, huh?"

"Sure. I've done it enough. I put the weird ones aside to get her opinion, anyway." She nodded toward a box that contained a pink pitcher and some small Coke bottles, with the drink still in them. "What should we charge for this?" She held up a small pitcher.

"I don't know. Fifty cents."

Katharine chuckled and wrote something that Nancy couldn't see on the sticker.

Nancy watched her work for a few moments, then said casually, "That prayer chain you have, are you the last person in the chain?"

Katharine paused from her work to look at her. "What do you mean?"

"Well, do you have anyone you call?"

"No. But there are a few of us who don't need to call anyone. Why?"

"I don't know. I've been thinking about something." She picked a bowl off the cart and cupped it in her hands. "The person who calls you, do they call other people too?"

"Sure, but only a couple, so it doesn't get to be a burden."

Nancy leaned forward, still clutching the bowl. "So the person who calls them must call a few people too, right?"

Katharine frowned. "I suppose so."

Nancy put the bowl back on the cart and leaned back, thinking. "How many of them do you know?"

"Who? You mean the people in the prayer chain?" Katharine pushed a strand of hair out of her eyes. "I suppose I know them all, at least a little. I mean, they're all—or mostly all—members of my church."

"Yeah, but do you know their position in the chain?"

"No, not really. I know Phyllis, but I don't even know who else she calls."

"Phyllis is the person who calls you?"

"Uh huh."

"What's her last name?"

"McGuinness."

"You wouldn't have her phone number, would you?"

"I have it at home, of course. But let me look."

Katharine stood up and arched her back to work the kinks out. Then she disappeared into the main part of the store. Nancy reached into the box and pulled out another glass bowl. She dusted the bottom off on her jeans and stuck a label on it. With the felt pen she wrote "$255.95." She had just put the bowl on the cart when Katharine reappeared, carrying her purse. Nancy looked up, innocently.

"I think I have it somewhere in here," Katharine said. She dug out a small appointment book and looked in the back. "Yes, here it is. Do you have something to write on?"

Nancy was still holding the pen. She looked around, and picked up a scrap of backing paper from the labels. "Shoot."

"It's 668-4543. Got that?"

"Yep."

Katharine put her purse on a shelf and sat back down on her stool. "So what's with all the questions about the prayer chain, anyway? And what was going on yesterday when you called? You said it was a long story, so out with it."

Nancy had known she would ask, but she still hesitated. Katharine was a friend, and at least she wouldn't laugh at her crazy notions.

"Well, I called from Good Sam hospital. I had just been visiting Mary Mowatt."

"Why? Was she in an accident? I didn't know she was sick."

"No. No accident." Nancy sighed. "Well, maybe it was. Listen, you need to keep this confidential. She tried to commit suicide."

Katharine stared at her, her mouth open.

"It's true," Nancy said, quietly. "I didn't get a chance to talk to her—she was asleep the whole time I was there."

"Oh no! But why?"

"I really don't know. John said he blames himself, and maybe he's right."

"How come?"

"Well, he was talking about leaving her."

Katharine rubbed her forehead. "So that's why you asked if the prayer chain had anything to do with John Mowatt."

"Yeah."

They sat in silence for a minute. The only sounds were the tapping of rain in the downspout and the hum of traffic in front of the store.

"But that doesn't make any sense," Katharine finally said.

"What?"

"The prayer chain. There can't be any connection."

"Why not?"

"Well, for one thing, we didn't pray for John or Mary Mowatt."

"Yes, but other parts of the chain may have. Who knows if the message got garbled."

Katharine shook her head. "I don't know."

Nancy shrugged.

"And besides," Katharine said, "there is no way a prayer chain can make something bad happen."

"How come?"

"Simple. God wouldn't let it."

Nancy didn't feel she was equipped to get into a theological argument, but she had thought about that problem. "Yeah, you're probably right. It wouldn't make sense. But then neither does much of the other weird stuff that's been going on around here."

"Oh, that's just coincidence. You know what they say—stuff happens."

"That's not exactly how I've heard it."

Katharine laughed. "Close enough, though." She reached down into the box and picked up another bowl. "How did someone ever collect this much junk?" She wiped it with a gray cloth. "That's terrible about Mary, though. Tell her I'll keep her in my prayers." She paused and looked up at Nancy. "If you trust me, that is."

***

A few customers were drinking coffee and talking when Nancy returned to the Fir Away. An Phat had prepared some of the ingredients for the dishes that could be done in advance, and was studying the menu.

"When you make Ruben sandwich, how much

corn beef do you use? How thick?" he asked.

"Oh, about this much," she said, making a narrow U with her thumb and forefinger. I usually give them the Thousand Island on the side, so they can put on as much as they want."

"Ah."

Nancy looked at him. He seemed to be about fifty. That would have put him as a child or teenager during the Vietnam war. Was he from the north or south? He could have been born in the states, for all she knew.

"If you like, we could feature a Vietnamese dish for our lunch special tomorrow," she said.

"No, Mrs. Mackay. It would not be wise to purchase the ingredients. Too much waste if not used regularly."

He turned to pick up an order slip that Jaime passed through the window. It occurred to Nancy that she could have insulted him. Maybe he didn't want to be typecast as a Vietnamese cook. With the French influence in Indochina, he could well have had formal training there in the culinary arts. She watched as he tossed a few strips of bacon on the griddle and sliced a tomato, moving with purpose and efficiency. She left the kitchen to help Jaime as lunch customers began drifting in.

***

Phyllis McGuinness was hard to reach. Nancy tried several times during the day, and only got an answering machine. She tried again in the evening, when Bruce was planted in front of the TV watching a baseball game and the kids were playing in the front yard in a break from the rain. The phone rang five times and Nancy was ready to hand up when a woman answered.

"Hello? Is this Phyllis McGuinness?"

"Yes…?" came the guarded response.

Nancy quickly mentioned her connection with Katharine, and that she was a local resident who owned the Fir Away Café. What was more difficult was giving a reasonable explanation for her interest in the prayer chain. She had considered posing as a member of another church who was interested in starting her own prayer chain. But she had an uneasy feeling about lying about it. She tried the truth.

"…so I'm just curious how it works, and whether it has anything to do with some of the events that have been happening lately."

"Well, I certainly hope it has something to do with events that happen. 'Ask and ye shall receive,' you know."

"Exactly. So, if I could ask, do you remember by any chance a prayer request in the last month or so for Mary Mowatt? Or anything having to do with John Mowatt?"

"No… I don't think so."

"Hmm." Nancy pulled a chair up to the kitchen table. "Well, do you know who else is in the chain? Like, where they are in it?"

"Well, I of course know the people I call. And the person who calls me."

"Can you tell me who they are?"

Phyllis hesitated.

"Don't worry, I won't pester them. I may try to reach a few of them to ask them about their experience in the chain, but that's all. It really is just personal curiosity."

"Well…"

"I'm sure Katharine will vouch for me. We've been friends for years."

"I guess there's no harm in it. None of us have anything to hide, you know."

"Sure."

Phyllis started reciting names, and Nancy scribbled furiously on a scrap of paper, occasionally stopping to ask for the spelling of a last name. Phyllis didn't offer any phone numbers, and Nancy decided not to press her luck.

"Oh, and a few weeks ago, Gretchen asked me to call the other people on her list. I think I may have kept the names. Hold on."

Gretchen Clymer was the person ahead of Phyllis, so her list would be the people—or at least some of the people, depending on the size of the chain—at Phyllis' level. An unexpected bit of luck. Nancy wrote the names down—there were only two besides Phyllis, and she knew—remotely—one of them.

"You know," Phyllis said, "you really ought to ask Pastor about this. I think he has the whole prayer chain list at his office. I should have thought of this when you first called."

"Yes, that's a good idea," Nancy said.

Phyllis gave her the office phone number, and Nancy paused, pretending to write it down. She had no intention of calling it.

"One more question," Nancy asked. "Do you remember a prayer request for Andy Brandon, probably some time last week?"

"Andy Brandon? No, but I know who he is, though. His mother was a classmate of mine, Cedar Creek

High, class of '61. What would we be praying for Andy for?"

"Are you sure you didn't get a request for him?"

"Yes." She paused. "Of course, I was in Hawaii last week, so I would have missed the messages then."

Nancy tapped the paper with her pencil and frowned. "But Katharine told me she got a prayer request that week. Where did it come from, if not from you?"

"Oh, I always tell Gretchen when I will be out of town, so she can cover for me."

"I see. So Gretchen just made your calls for you."

"Actually, she usually passes them on to someone else."

"Okay," Nancy said, trying to keep the impatience out of her voice. "And who was that?"

"My dear, do you think I'm clairvoyant? I haven't a clue."

6

Jaime Saldivar was late leaving for work. He ran down the stairs from the apartment he shared with his mother and threw open the door of his battered Ford pickup truck. He tossed his coat on the passenger seat and jammed the lap belt into the lock. Nothing happened when he twisted the key in the ignition. He jiggled the shift lever with his left hand while holding the key, and the engine coughed into life.

Rush hour was pretty much over, so the traffic wasn't too bad. After a few miles on arterial streets, he pulled onto the four lane highway to Cedar Creek. The radio wasn't working—he had forgotten to stick the coat hanger back into the antenna hole the last time he had washed the truck, a month ago—but he made up for it by belting out the words to a country song. A car a half mile ahead of him was driving erratically, so Jaime eased his foot off the gas pedal and kept his distance.

He was late because he had slept in. His grandmother just wasn't doing too well. She was out of the hospital again and back in the nursing home, but it was only a matter of time. Her mind was sharp, but her body was giving up on her, a conspiracy of the years. Whether it was the medication or simple loneliness, she hadn't been able to sleep and had insisted he stay late. The TV had been on, and they hadn't talked much, but it was past midnight before she let him kiss her wrinkled cheek and drive back through the empty streets to his apartment.

He glanced at his watch and realized he was due at the restaurant five minutes ago. He let his speed creep up to 64 mph. The road noise rang through the sheet metal of the truck cab and water hissed in the wheel wells as the tires sliced through the puddles in the worn grooves of the asphalt. Jaime tapped his left foot in time to his song. Ah dono wah ah luv ya baybay but ah dooo, he sang. His mother would have to work late again tonight, so he would have dinner with his grandmother at the nursing home. He needed his paycheck soon, since her Medicare and social security payments were falling well short of what the nursing home was charging.

The car ahead had drifted into the left lane. Jaime pressed the accelerator and began to pass on the right. Without warning, the car moved back into his lane. The road had narrowed, with a guardrail on his right. Jaime leaned on the horn, remembering too late that it hadn't worked for years, and hit the gas to try to pull ahead. The engine groaned; at highway speed the acceleration was sluggish. As he pulled ahead, the car hit him just behind his door, breaking the grip of the back tires and pushing him into a slow spin. Jaime yelled and countersteered, keeping the front of the truck more or less straight. But it was drifting to the right, and the tail end slammed into the guardrail. It bounced back hard, flipping the truck into a roll. It came to a stop, upside down, on the grass median between the lanes. Jaime hung, unconscious, from his lap belt, the dented top of the cab an inch from his head.

***

Mary was home, but her doctor had told her to rest another day before returning to work. An Phat was pleased to be able to work there, he said, and Nancy was relieved that he was still available. She helped him prepare some of the ingredients for the lunch selection, and brewed a couple pots of coffee.

At 11:00 Nancy realized that Jaime was an hour late. He was usually so reliable, in spite of his late night trysts. She went back into the kitchen and searched her desk for the phone book. His home number was on a loose sheet of paper stuck in the back of the book. She called, but there was no answer. She tried Sally, but day care was a problem, and she had promised to spend some time volunteering in her oldest daughter's classroom. So Nancy was on her own.

The lunch crowd was light—a mixed blessing—and An Phat even helped by carrying some of the meals out to the customers. She called Bruce to ask him to deal with dinner for the kids, and she worked on into the evening shift. A high school girl came in at 5:30 to help wait on tables, and by 8:30 the place was empty.

She tried calling Jaime, but again there was no answer, and no way to leave a message. She locked up the café, figuring that he would simply show up the next day.

But Mary was in first. Nancy sat down with her over a cup of coffee.

"So. How are you doing?"

Mary pressed her lips together, and Nancy was afraid she was going to cry. But she grinned, instead.

"I'm doing great," she said. She leaned forward. "I know it was a crazy thing to do, but in some ways, I wish I had done it sooner."

"What, kill yourself?" It sounded blunt, but Nancy

couldn't believe what she was hearing.

"Oh. Yeah, it would have been a bummer if John hadn't found me. But ever since…I guess I needed something like that to get him out of his funk."

"Yes, but isn't that sort of extreme?"

Mary shrugged. "Maybe. But what was the alternative? Anyway, John's been really good to me; he isn't talking anymore about moving out. Even our sex life is, uh, better." She seemed to blush a little. "But hey, I'm sorry for leaving you stuck like that. I feel bad about that, more than anything else."

"Oh, we managed. I was able to get a cook from a temp agency. But I'm so glad you're back, and you're okay."

The phone rang. "Hold on," Nancy said. She picked up the phone on the counter. It was Jaime.

"Hey there, amigo," Nancy said. "I missed you yesterday."

"Yeah, I know. Sorry about that. I'm afraid I can't make it in today, either."

"Oh?"

"Yeah. You see, I'm in the hospital."

"Oh no! Why?"

"I got in a car wreck on the way to work yesterday. Totaled the truck. I don't know what I'm going to do about it. I had insurance, but the insurance agent said they won't give me more than $500 for it, 'cause it was so old. But my uncle, he says he might sell me his old Corsica. It doesn't look like much, but at least it runs. Of course, I wouldn't be able to--"

"Hold on, Jaime. Forget your truck. What about you? If you're in a hospital you must be injured. So what happened?"

"Oh, somebody side-swiped me, and I guess the truck rolled. It wasn't my fault, but the other person, they never even stopped. They were driving kind of funny, so maybe they were stoned or falling asleep at the wheel or something like that. There was a guy behind me, saw the whole thing, and he pulled over and called 911. I guess he told the sheriff that the other guy side-swiped me. That's what I hear, at least. I was out cold at the time. At least they didn't give me a ticket or anything. Didn't even charge me for towing the truck. Of course, it won't do me much good anyway. I liked that truck. I had just put on some new tires. Of course, they weren't really new, they were re-treads, but they still cost me—"

"Jaime. One more time. Are you all right?"

"Me? Sure. Well, I'm sort of bruised up. Look like I've been in a bar room fight, I guess. And my leg's broken. But I'm all right."

Nancy leaned against the wall and stared at the ceiling. "Who is it?" Mary called from the kitchen. Nancy shook her head.

"And how bad is the break, Jaime?"

"Oh, not bad at all. Just a simple fracture, I think they call it. The docs even have it in a walking cast, so I'll be able to come to work tomorrow, no problem. Itches like crazy, though."

"Listen, don't come in tomorrow, even if they let you out of the hospital."

"Okay. But--"

"No, listen to me. After going through something like that, you need some rest. Don't push yourself. Mary's back today, and we'll do fine. I'm just glad you're okay, that you didn't get hurt worse. You just take it easy. Do you hear me?"

"Yes, mother." He chuckled. "I have a parade of girl friends coming in to sign my cast. So it could be worse, yes?"

"You just take it easy. What hospital are you at?"

"Mount Hood. But they're letting me out this afternoon. My mom's getting off work early to pick me up. I'll be fine, really. I just wanted to call to let you know I couldn't come in."

"Well, thanks. I'll call you tomorrow, okay?"

"All right. Adiós, boss."

Nancy told Mary what had happened, then called Sally Dupree to see if she could come in. Sally hesitated, and told Nancy she would call back. When she did, she said she could cover for Jaime, but she would need to bring her youngest, Christopher, with her for a few hours until her baby-sitter was free. That suited Nancy fine. Maybe I can let him run the business for a while, Nancy thought. A four-year-old couldn't make a worse mess of it.

Both Mary and Jaime had been using sick leave, so Nancy would have to pay them in addition to what she paid the temp agency and Sally. It was, she knew, unusual to have sick leave in that line of work, but she had always thought that was unfair. Besides, she wanted to discourage her staff from coming in when they were actually sick. The last thing she needed was an outbreak of disease that was attributed to her café.

At least she didn't have to cover the medical costs. Mary was covered by John's Teamsters policy. Jaime was another matter; she didn't have any idea how Jaime was going to pay his hospital bill. Probably the Oregon Health Plan, designed for people out of work or otherwise unemployable. Or waiters in restaurants, she thought ruefully.

"Hey, why the somber look?"

Isaac had come bursting into the café, followed by Katherine.

"Oh, hi you two. I was just thinking. A rare event, so you probably don't know what I look like when I do."

"Ha ha." They sat at the counter. Isaac pulled off his hat and shook out his pony tail. He had blue and pink paint on his knuckles and a smudge of charcoal on a wrinkled cheek.

Katharine craned her neck to look into the kitchen. "Mary, it's good to see you back," she called out.

Mary smiled and waved through the opening.

"Now my problem is I'm missing Jaime," Nancy said.

"Yeah, it seems a little dull in here," Isaac said, looking around. "What happened, his wardrobe get depleted or something?"

"No, he got hurt in a car accident."

"Uh oh. Is he okay?"

"Broken leg. Some bruises, I guess."

"I'm not surprised," Katharine said. "The roads sure have been slick. Not like in the winter, but people are usually more careful when they're wet. The roads, I mean. But now, they've been wet so long, people drive like normal. This morning I saw someone make a turn too fast, onto 3rd Street, and they almost wrapped their car around a phone pole."

"Say," Nancy said slowly, "there wasn't any mention of Jaime in the prayer chain, was there?"

"What are you talking about?" Isaac said.

"No," Katharine said. "I hate to mess up your theory, but it sounds like it was just an accident."

"What theory?" Isaac said.

"Nancy thinks that some of the messages in the prayer chain get garbled, and bad things happen."

"Well, I'm not ready to give up on it," Nancy said. "See, they prayed about Andy Brandon's kidney stone <u>before</u> he got it, and then he really got one. And," she leaned forward and lowered her voice, "and I think it might have had something to do with Mary and John. And maybe some other stuff too."

"Hmm," Isaac said. "Sounds like the Twilight Zone to me."

"Don't Jews think prayers come true sometimes?" Nancy asked.

"Ha. Not for this one. Bad stuff, now that's another thing. That happens to us all the time. Usually because we've fouled up in some way, took too many steps on the Sabbath, chopped the meat on the wrong plate, that sort of thing. Last I checked there are a few hundred things we can do wrong a day. I gave up trying to avoid them." He rubbed some stubble on his chin. "I'm okay on the commandments, I suppose. 'Least I haven't killed anyone recently. Coveting, now, that's another thing. I think that's still on the list."

Katharine turned to look at Isaac and shook her head slowly. "So did you ever call Phyllis?" she asked Nancy.

"Yeah. She gave me a few names. By the way, she said she was in Hawaii when Andy got sick. Said that somebody called you in her place. Who was it?"

Katharine thought for a moment. "I really can't remember. By the way, what's Jaime's last name?"

"Saldivar."

"You know, I read a sci-fi story once about a kid

who would dream things, and the dreams would come true," Isaac said. "Like, his parents died in a terrible car accident after they punished him for something, and his teacher got stung by a scorpion, and a new bicycle appeared in his garage. After a while, someone caught on to it, and they tried to figure out how to get him to dream what they wanted him to. Hey, what's the matter?"

Nancy glanced at Katharine, who looked stricken. "What is it?"

"We did have a prayer request. Two days ago. Not for Jaime. But for Amy. Amy Salveter."

"Oh no." Nancy felt the hair on her neck tingle. "What was the prayer for?"

"Healing." Katharine's voice caught. "She had been in a car accident."

***

"How long do we have to stay for, Mom?"

Nancy glanced over. Indigo looked small in the passenger seat, her legs almost straight as she sat. "Not long. Thanks for coming with me, hon."

Bruce was still at a dinner meeting with one of his bank customers—a dealer of farm tractors and implements—and the older kids were playing at a neighbor's house. It was 7:00 but the sun was still high, trying to shine through a hole in the clouds.

Nancy pulled up in front of a small 1920s craftsman-style house with a full front porch and thick columns painted milk white. Indigo held her hand as she rang the doorbell.

After a long wait, the door opened.

"Mrs. Clymer?"

"Yes?"

"I'm Nancy Mackay. I called you earlier. Phyllis McGuinness gave me your name—you know, with the church's prayer chain."

"Oh! Yes! Come in."

They walked across a thick shag rug that would have felt luxurious if it weren't for the fact that the path from the door was covered by a clear plastic runner. Gretchen Clymer motioned them with a quick flick of her wrist to an overstuffed sofa with a dark floral pattern. The couch, too, was covered by a thick plastic cover. They sat, and waited for Mrs. Clymer to take her seat on an old rocker—also carefully preserved under plastic. The smell of fried chicken hung in the air, mixed with a faint odor of menthol.

"And what is your name, dear?"

"Indigo."

"Pardon?"

Nancy whispered, "Louder."

"Indigo. My name is Indigo."

"Really? Like the color? Is that what you said?"

"Uh huh."

"I see. Well, that's a nice name. I suppose not that different from Violet or Scarlet, eh?"

"No, scarlet is kind of red."

"Those are other names, hon," Nancy said.

"Oh." Indigo said.

Mrs. Clymer folded her hands and blinked. Her thin hair had been curled in the recent past but now floated around her head in wild white wisps.

"So," she said.

"We really don't want to take much of your time, ma'am," Nancy said quickly. "You see, I'm very interested in your prayer chain. I just wanted to ask you a few questions about it. For example--"

"I've been a part of it for many, many years, you know. Probably since before you were born. Haven't missed a week in over forty years. Of course, there are some weeks when we don't get a request at all, but not very many. On those weeks I fill in my own requests, and pray for those. Sometimes I don't even have anything to pray for but I do anyway. It says in Romans that we do not know what we ought to pray for, but the Spirit himself intercedes for us with groans that words cannot express. Are you familiar with the passage, dear?"

"Uh, no, I don't think so. What I was curious about—"

"Well, I think there is truth in it, but most of the time we do have things and people to pray for, and so that's what we do."

Nancy waited for a moment to see if she was finished, or just catching her breath.

"Here's a question I have, though. How do you know the prayer request is accurate?"

"Is what, dear?"

"Accurate. How do know the prayer request you get is the right one?"

"I don't know what you mean. I don't think the other people would lie, do you now? No, I know them all very well, and I believe they are all good Christians."

"I'm sure they are, Mrs. Clymer, but isn't it possible that if the message gets passed from person to person, it can start to get distorted? I mean, it wouldn't be intentional, but maybe somebody doesn't hear it quite right, or forgets exactly what the message was, or writes it down wrong. You know?"

Mrs. Clymer just rocked and stared at her. Nancy wasn't sure she had heard.

"I'm not saying it would be intentional," Nancy repeated.

"Well, I don't know," Mrs. Clymer finally said. "It doesn't seem likely to me. I'm quite good at directions. If somebody tells me how to find an address, why, I write it down. And then I follow the directions, and always end up where I'm supposed to be. Of course, I don't drive much now, especially at night or in bad weather. And my, hasn't the weather been extraordinary, don't you think?"

"Uh, yes."

"So you see, if I can follow directions that someone tells me, don't you think I should be able to follow a prayer request, quite accurately in fact?"

"I'm sure you do, ma'am. But it's different. Suppose a chain of people gave directions. What starts off as, say, two thirty four Elm Street might turn into two forty three Elm Street, then two forty three Maple Street, then forty three May Pole Street, and so on."

"Now why would a group of people pass on directions like that? I'm always careful to get the directions from someone who really knows the address."

"Exactly! You go to the source so you don't rely on somebody passing on wrong information."

Mrs. Clymer closed her eyes and her chin dropped. Was she suddenly taking a nap?

"Mrs. Clymer?"

Suddenly her head snapped up. "It isn't so much that, dear. I have found that some people are not very good at directions. For instance, many people have a hard time knowing east from west. They are better at north and south, but they get mixed up between east and west. Do you know why that is?"

"Umm, no…"

"I have a theory about it."

"Uh huh. Getting back to the prayer chain, do you know the names of some of the other people in the chain? Like, the person who--"

"My theory is that people stand on their feet, with their head on top, so it is easy to tell north from south. North is top, where our head is, and south is bottom, where our feet are. But we're…what's the word?" She paused, rocking slowly. "Yes, symmetrical. We're symmetrical from side to side. If west is left and east is right, we have to stop and think about it, because our mirror images look just like we do. Our left side looks like our right side. Did you ever wonder about that?"

"What?"

"Why our reflection in a mirror is flipped side to side but not top to bottom? How does the mirror know?"

"I never thought about it," Nancy said.

There was a twinkle in Mrs. Clymer's eyes. "Well, try it some time. You can even lie on your side in front of a mirror, and your left and right sides will still be switched around, but your head and feet will still be the same, even though they are now side to side and your arms are top and bottom. A mystery, isn't it?"

Indigo started looking around the room. She wants to try it, Nancy thought.

"It's like a thermos," Mrs. Clymer continued.

"Pardon?"

"Yes, a thermos. If you put something hot in, it keeps it hot. If you put something cold in, it keeps it cold. How does it know? A stove makes everything hot, and refrigerator keeps everything cold, but a thermos knows what you want hot and what you want cold. What a marvelous invention!"

She was looking at Indigo, who in turn was looking at the ceiling, deep in thought. The old gal's playing with us, Nancy thought.

"Yeah. How <u>does</u> it know, Mom?"

"It's insulated, hon. It has a vacuum in it so that it doesn't conduct heat well."

"Huh?"

"I'll explain later."

Mrs. Clymer moved her jaws a few times, adjusting her dentures. "What was it you were asking, dear?"

"Oh, yes. I wanted to know the names of some of the other people in the prayer chain."

"So you trust me to get the names right, eh?"

"Of course." Nancy looked at her, questioning.

"Hah!" Mrs. Clymer barked. She rocked forward a few times, building up momentum, and on the third rock she stood up, keeping a hand on the bobbing chair to steady herself. "My, my," she said, and shuffled into the kitchen. Nancy heard a drawer open, and the ringing sounds of pots and pans.

Indigo started swinging her legs, bumping her heels into the front of the sofa. Nancy put a hand lightly on her knee to stop her, and wondered if she should go into the kitchen to see what Mrs. Clymer was up to. Nancy's elbow and forearm were sticking to the plastic on the sofa's armrest. The old bird had to be in her mid- or late-eighties. The furniture would easily outlive her, so what was with all the plastic?

Mrs. Clymer came back in, humming a one-note tune and clutching a few sheets of paper. She let herself drop back into the rocking chair. "I found them!" she announced.

"What's that?"

"The names of the people in the prayer chain!"

"All of them?" Nancy couldn't believe it.

Mrs. Clymer didn't seem to hear. She resumed humming and started leafing through the sheets, nodding to herself.

"Could I take a look at them?" Nancy asked.

"Eh?" Mrs. Clymer pulled out one of the sheets and looked up. "Edna Scoville. Now there's a fine person."

"Uh, where is she in the prayer chain?" Nancy asked. She fished a notebook and pen out of her purse.

"She was one of the people I would call," the old lady said absently.

Was? "Why don't you still call her?"

"Oh, she passed away, God rest her soul."

"How long ago?"

Mrs. Clymer paused. "Five, ten years ago. I don't really remember. She was old. And here's another one. Franklin Gooding. Now there was a real gentleman. He's dead too, of course."

Nancy let the pen and paper rest on her lap. "Mrs. Clymer, how many of those names are of people in the prayer chain now?"

She looked up and blinked. "Oh, hardly any. I suppose I've outlasted most of them." A few of the sheets slipped out of her fingers and sailed to the floor. "Now, let me see…" She looked around for the missing sheets.

"Could you pick them up for her?" Nancy whispered to Indigo. Her daughter, glad of the opportunity to move, launched herself from the sofa and scurried to collect the papers.

"Ah, here it is!"

"What's that?"

"The people I call these days. I know it's the right one by the tomato stain on the corner. You see, I was making some spaghetti sauce when I was called a few weeks ago. No, maybe it was a month or two ago." She shook her head. "Anyway, I put my mixing spoon down right here, on the corner of the paper. Not very neat of me, was it?"

"What are the names?"

"Yes." She tilted her head back to get the paper into focus. "Phyllis you know, of course." She scanned the list and read off two more names as Nancy scribbled them down.

"Is that it?"

"Well. It's quite enough. Even with three, if we have any news to share, why, it can take three evenings just to pass on one prayer request. My heavens, I don't know what I would do with more."

"And who calls you?"

"Ed does, most of the time."

Nancy made a note. "What's his last name."

"Oh, I don't really remember. It's some sort of Scottish name."

"A Scottish name." She tapped her knee with the pen. "Well, here's another question. Phyllis McGuinness said that you got someone to make her calls when she was gone to Hawaii a few weeks ago. Could you tell me who that was?"

"Hawaii! That's where she went! I was trying to remember that the other day, when I was talking with my granddaughter. I might have said Fiji or Tahiti by mistake. My granddaughter has spent some time in the south Pacific, you know."

"Uh huh. So while Phyllis was in Hawaii, who made her calls?"

Mrs. Clymer's brow wrinkled for a few moments, then she closed her eyes.

"Sorry," she said, looking up. "Could have been anybody. I sometimes get somebody from the congregation who isn't even in the prayer chain—good practice for them, I always say. I used to call on Fritz Mann. He grumbled, but was still a good sport about it."

"Could he have been the one you asked this time?"

"Oh, no. He's gone too, I'm sorry to say."

This was turning into a wild goose chase. "Okay. Mrs. Clymer, I don't want to take much more of your time. Do you by any chance know how many people are ahead of you in the chain?"

"Ahead of me?"

"Yes. The person who calls Ed—is that your pastor, or someone else in the congregation."

"I don't really know. Haven't thought much about that. I would say many of the prayers come straight from God himself, but then, we do get some strange ones some times."

"Like what?" Nancy asked, suddenly interested.

"Well, just the other week, someone wanted us to pray so that her daughter would do well on her chemistry test."

"What's so strange about that?"

Mrs. Clymer laughed. "Can't you just hear God, up there in heaven with his angels, saying, 'Help me out here, little girl. Why don't you try studying!'"

As she drove home with Indigo in the front seat, Nancy despaired of ever getting a handle on names and shape of the prayer chain. If there were five layers in the chain, and each person called three others… She did the math in her head. One plus three plus nine plus twenty-seven plus…

"What are you thinking about, Mom?"

"Arithmetic. What's twenty-seven times three?"

"Don't be silly, Mom. They don't teach us that in kindergarten. I can count to twenty-seven though." She started quietly going through the numbers.

Eighty-one, Nancy thought as she pulled into her driveway. Twenty-seven times three had to be the same as nine times nine. So altogether, there could be a hundred and twenty one people in the chain. And she just had a fraction of the names, and hardly any of the structure. Maybe I should pray about it, she thought, and laughed to herself.

Whether or not that simple thought sufficed as a complete prayer, it was answered the next day.

7

The call came in the morning, while Nancy was going over some work details with Sally. Jaime was home from the hospital, but Nancy had called the night before to make sure he wasn't tempted to come in to work. One of his normal duties, between the lunch and dinner crowds, was to make sure the restroom was clean and the trash can was emptied. It wasn't the most pleasant job, but he never complained. Sally had always seemed to avoid it, and Nancy was tempted to just do it herself, but then it occurred to her that Sally was probably making more money at the café than she was,...so she might as well earn it.

Mary handed her the phone. "It's for you."

"Hello, Nancy speaking."

"Hi Nancy. This is Dave Montgomery. I'm the pastor here at the Cedar Creek Community Church. I heard you've been asking some questions about our prayer chain."

Nancy didn't know what to say. Instead of replying, she felt behind her for a chair at the nearest table, and pulled it toward her. She sat down and closed her eyes.

"Are you still there?"

"Yes, I am. Sorry." Some of the members of the congregation must have talked to him. It was a possibility she had been aware of, but had put out of her mind. It wasn't that she had anything to hide. But she knew she would be completely outmatched in any sort of theological discussion. And there were some questions that would inevitably come up, and she didn't want to face them.

"Anyhow, as I was saying, I understand that you're curious about the prayer chain. I'd be glad to talk to you about it. I realize you have a business to run there, so I would be willing to meet with you there. Say in a half hour?"

He's willing to <u>meet</u> with me? Nancy thought. It made it sound like union negotiations. "Yeah, that would be fine. I'll be here."

"Good. See you then."

Nancy put the phone down and sat for a moment. His voice had seemed calm and friendly. Maybe it wouldn't be so bad after all.

Nancy looked around the restaurant, wondering how it would look to a minister. A couple of her Far Side cartoons on the wall had jokes about hell. But even Katharine had found them funny. And what about the music in the CD player? Nothing really wrong there—it was a family restaurant, after all.

You're being silly, she told herself. He wouldn't care what was on the wall. He wouldn't ask her if she and Bruce had slept together before they were married, or whether she tried pot when she was in college. Still, though… She paced around, straightening the furniture and wiping the counter clean.

A while later a man—much younger than she had expected—came into the café. He was tall, and bent his head forward as if to de-emphasize his height. He's been here before, Nancy realized. Enough times that she knew him as "Dave," although she had never guessed that he was a preacher. That brought back another rush of thoughts—had she said something inappropriate, or cursed when she had spilled a drink?

"So you're that Dave Montgomery," was all she said, and held out her hand.

"Yeah, that's me," he said. His grip was firm, and his hand was wet from the drizzle outside.

"So, do you want to just sit out here?" Nancy said, and immediately regretted it. Where else would they sit, in the kitchen or behind the counter?

"Sure," he said, still standing.

"Uh, okay, let's go ahead and use this one." She pulled a chair from the corner table for him, and she moved around to take the opposite side, so she could see the café and any other customers that came in. She folded her hands and waited for him.

"So how's your business doing?" he said. "Is this the first restaurant you've owned?"

"Yes. It's doing all right. Well, I miss the tourists. At least their money. But the locals have been pretty loyal."

He nodded. A few strands of his straight black hair fell onto his forehead. "What made you—"

"Oh! What a poor host I'm being. Can I get you some coffee, or anything else? Or do people in your church even drink coffee?"

"Sure we do. You're thinking of the Mormons. Well, come to think of it, I've been to a few Lutheran church events and I've wondered if it was coffee they were serving, or just warm water." He grinned at her, and she allowed herself a giggle. "And yes, come to think of it, I could use a cup. Black, if you've got it."

She sprang up and filled two mugs from an air pot. He took a sip, carefully to avoid burning his tongue.

"Umm, it's good." He put the mug down and looked at her. "So, what made you decide to start the business?"

"Oh, I don't know. It's something I've always wanted to do. The kids are all in school now—well, at least school age, they're on vacation now—and I just needed something to keep myself busy."

"You like to cook?"

"No, strangely enough. I mean, I don't mind it, but I don't think I'm that great at it. That's why I have Mary." She tilted her head toward the kitchen. "And Ernesto. What I really wanted was a place where people would feel welcome, where they could come in and talk, maybe have some coffee or an Italian soda or a meal, but not feel rushed. I do like seeing the people that come in here, and sometimes it gets packed, even mid-morning every once in a while, and the windows steam up and the conversations get so loud that you can hardly hear the espresso machine. That's when I like it best."

He smiled and nodded and took another sip of coffee. He was wearing a tweed coat and a blue oxford cloth shirt and looked more like a prep school teacher—or student—than a preacher.

"And what about you?" she asked. "What made you decide to become a minister?"

He considered the question for a moment. "Maybe for some of the same reasons. Every few months we have a potluck in our fellowship hall, or a picnic outside when the weather is nice, and I love seeing the folks in the congregation having a good time, comfortable with each other and laughing and talking. Or when the teenagers in our youth group just hang out and act like goofy kids, when you know there's so much pressure in high school to be cool. And for me, the best is when we have a worship service, and I hardly have to do anything, but can just sit back and enjoy the other members of the congregation as they take on the various roles in the service. That doesn't happen often, though, since I have to at least do the message most Sundays. That's my job, though, so I guess its okay."

"Yeah, I know what you mean. When it's the way I like it best in here, I'm usually so busy I can't really enjoy it."

"The tough part about being a business owner, huh?"

"That's about it."

Dave looked around the café. "You've done a good job with this place, you know."

He's smooth, Nancy thought. He probably had to take psychology in seminary.

"Thanks," she said.

"So." He propped his chin on his knuckles and looked into her eyes. "You're a friend of Katharine Regan."

"Yeah. She was an aide when I used to be a teacher. We've known each other for years." Nancy wanted to keep talking, to steer the conversation, but the words didn't come.

"And something she said made you curious about the prayer chain."

"Yes. Well, not just that. But until she mentioned it, I didn't know there was one, or how it worked."

"Tell me what interests you about it." It was a soft

question, like Mr. Rogers interviewing a young child.

"Do you want more coffee?"

He broke eye contact and looked into his mug. "No, I'm fine, thanks." He waited.

"Okay." She sighed. "I guess it first got my attention because of a person I know was having an affair. When I mentioned her name, and the name of the person she was having the affair with, Katharine said the names sounded a lot like a couple that had just been mentioned in the prayer chain."

He raised his eyebrows but said nothing.

"I know that doesn't sound like much. But then other things started happening." She continued, telling him about the prayer for someone who sounded like John Mowatt who had walked out on his wife, about Andy Brandon's kidney stone, about Jaime's accident.

When she finished he sat quietly for a moment. "You know, I would take a refill on the coffee now, if the offer's still open."

Nancy started to get up, but Sally carried over the pot.

"Want me to warm them up?" she asked.

"Sure. Thanks."

When she had left, the young pastor scratched his chin thoughtfully. "So only one of those had exactly the same name, right? I mean, in the other cases, the prayer was for someone else."

"Well, yes."

"Do you think it could just be a coincidence?"

"Yeah, it could."

He waited for her to say something else. "But you don't think it is," he said after a few moments.

"I really don't know. But here's the thing. When

Katharine got the prayer request for Andy Brandon, the person who called her wasn't Phyllis, the person who normally calls. It was someone else. So there could be a part of the chain where the message is getting especially garbled."

"Ah. I see."

A few customers had drifted in. Nancy surveyed the room to see if anyone had been waiting long. Sally seemed to have it under control.

"I know it sounds crazy," she said. "Maybe there's nothing to it."

"Probably. But you may be on to something."

"Really?"

"Maybe. See, everyone has a gift that they can use in ministry. For some, it's music, or singing. For others, it may be the gift of serving others, like social workers or missionaries. For some, it's teaching. For some, healing." He looked at the door as a young couple came in. "For others, it could be hospitality. Making people feel welcome. Do you know what I mean?"

"Yes…"

"And some people have an especially powerful gift of prayer. Sometimes they're called 'intercessors,' since they intercede with God on someone else's behalf. Of course, I believe that Jesus is the ultimate intercessor, but some people may have the gift too, at a more human level."

"So you think someone in the prayer chain might be like that?"

"I don't know. It's possible."

"But, uh…" she was going to call him by his first name, then wondered if people were allowed to address ministers that way. "But Phyllis said something that you would know a lot more about than me. Would God really let bad things happen, just because an intercessor prayed them?"

"Hmmm. The short answer is, 'no.' But there may be something else going on. You didn't ask the bigger question."

Nancy looked at him and shrugged. If it was a game of theological trivial pursuit, she was doomed before she started.

He chuckled. "Do you like the Doors?"

"The old rock band?"

He nodded.

"Well…no, not really. My husband Bruce does, though. Why?"

"See, I'm a real Doors fan."

"Really? No offense, but you seem too young…and…"

"And it's not exactly Christian music? Yeah, you're right about that. When I was a young teenager, well before I ever thought about going into the ministry, I stumbled across some old vinyl records that my dad had stored in our basement. The Doors were in the box. I just liked the music, and didn't really think too much about the lyrics. But there's this one song where Jim Morrison sort of tells this story. He says, 'when I was in seminary—'"

"What?"

"Right, it's hard to picture. Jim Morrison as a pastor. I have to assume that a lot of his songs had fictional lyrics, don't you think? Anyway, he says, 'When I was in seminary they put forth the proposition that you can petition the Lord with prayer. Petition the Lord with prayer. Petition the Lord with prayer.' And then he screams, 'You cannot petition the Lord with prayer!' And, strangely enough, years later I found myself in seminary and wondered about this very question."

Nancy leaned forward, fascinated. "What was the answer?"

He put his hands out, palms up, as if he had just proved a math theorem. "Jim Morrison was wrong. At least, according to scripture he was. You see, it says all through scripture that God wants us to bring our needs and wants to him in prayer. The sermon on the mount in Mathew is probably the best-known example—you know, where Jesus says, 'Ask, and you shall receive,' but there are plenty of other examples in both the old and the new testament."

"Yeah, but doesn't it say we're not supposed to be selfish, or greedy? What if we ask for things, like winning the lottery, or a new car, or even for a promotion at work?"

"Bingo!"

"Huh?"

"That's exactly the point. That's exactly the struggle I had in seminary." His eyes narrowed as if he were sizing her up. "You haven't been to divinity school, have you?"

"Me?" She laughed. "Far from it."

"Hmm. Well, anyway, you hit the nail on the head. The interesting thing is, for the most part, scripture doesn't say anything about that. God actually encourages us to petition him with prayer, and he doesn't seem to mind what it is we pray about. Jesus even included the words, "Give us this day our daily bread' in his model prayer, so apparently it's okay to ask God to take care of our basic human needs and appetites. Notice he didn't even include the word 'please.' It's just, 'Give me,' like a young child would say."

"Okay, then why doesn't it work more often?"

"You mean, why haven't I—or a lot of other Christians—won the lottery, things like that?"

"Uh huh." She nodded.

"Well, that's another story. I thought about that too in seminary, when it was hot out and I had been playing softball, and decided to pray for a can of cold beer. The can never materialized in my hand like I wanted it to. I had to sneak into town for that. But maybe that <u>was</u> the answer to the prayer."

"How do you figure?"

"Well, they had some yuppie fern bars, but I would usually go to a tavern. And I would get into some pretty deep discussions with some of the guys there about philosophy and people's souls."

"Probably helped that they'd had a few beers."

He cocked his head at her and gave a short laugh. "Could be. But you've seen the kids wearing WWJD bracelets? I asked myself, 'What would Jesus do?' and the answer was, he'd be out talking to folks. Sure, he preached in the synagogues, and had people follow him up a mountain, but most of the time he was in the middle of their lives, where they lived, where there were even tax collectors and prostitutes." He took a sip of coffee, then held it to warm his hand. His narrow fingers almost encircled the mug. "One of the guys I met in the tavern actually entered the seminary. He's a pastor in Wenatchee now."

"Wow."

"Yeah. But that's another story. What was the point I was trying to make?" He scratched his chin. "Oh.

See, I came to the conclusion that God really wants us to be talking to him all the time—sharing our thoughts, our worries, our needs, and our joy. Of course, he knows all those things anyway, but I think he wants us to acknowledge his presence, and be conscious of it all the time. So even if we're asking for things that may be a little selfish, or that aren't good for us, at least we're making the effort to talk to him. He prefers that over indifference, at least that's what I came to understand."

Something he had said made Nancy feel uneasy. She wasn't sure what it was.

"So what about the 'ask and you will receive' business?" she said. "How come the can of beer <u>didn't</u> appear in your hand?"

"Well, I think we have to have faith that our prayers <u>are</u> answered, but maybe in ways we don't expect. We have to trust that God really does know what's best for us."

"But what about parents whose child gets cancer, or gets hit by a car. How can that be an answer to a prayer?"

"That's a problem, true. C.S. Lewis tackled it in one of his books. All I can say is, sometimes it <u>is</u> very hard to see why God sets that kind of path for us. Maybe it's a test, like in Job."

They sat for a minute without talking. A few more customers had come in. Nancy had a fleeting thought that she should get up and help Sally, and easily pushed it away. She was comfortable sitting here with the young pastor, and the realization of that fact astonished her.

"Want anything to eat? You can have an early lunch."

"No, thanks," he said. "I have to meet someone."

"Are you married?"

"No. Not yet. Do you have any sisters that are available?"

She laughed. Both of her sisters were older. One was a widow, but so set in her ways that Nancy figured she would never re-marry. The other was a housewife in Las Vegas, with a couple of kids in college. Definitely not his type. Then it occurred to her that he may have meant it as a compliment.

"Haven't come across any cute parishioners, huh?"

"As a matter of fact, I have. Sort of a problem there, though."

"Why? Doesn't your church allow you to…"

"To marry one of the flock? No, it's technically okay. But it can get kind of awkward. You know, I'm supposed to be ministering to them, not hitting on them."

She laughed again.

"Seriously, it's a problem. See, where else am I going to find someone? I spend almost all my time with my own congregation members. And it wouldn't look good to hang out in singles bars, would it?"

She shrugged. "We don't really have any of those in Cedar Creek, anyway. But hey, there's always the Internet. You know, 'View photos of singles in your area.'"

"Ha. Do you think all those 'singles' are really single?"

She looked at him, puzzled. "You mean…? Well, I'll be. Hey, you're supposed to be the innocent one here."

He chuckled. "Jesus told us we should be shrewd about the world."

"He did?"

"Sure. Look it up. Luke 16."

She considered it. "Okay, I will." She wasn't sure they even had a Bible in the house. "All this time, you've been distracting me, haven't you?"

His dark eyebrows lifted. "How so?"

"The prayer chain. You really don't want me to pursue it, do you?"

He held her eyes and reached into his coat pocket. He handed her some papers, neatly folded in thirds.

"What is this?" she asked.

He said nothing, so she unfolded the thin stack. It was a diagram, like an organization chart, with names and phone numbers.

"The prayer chain!"

"Yep."

Her eyes followed the tree downward, and it branched near the bottom of the page, with letters in circles, A, B, C. She shuffled through the other pages, and the chain continued, with more letters showing how the branches connected to more pages. Some of the names were typed, but most were written in a neat script, with some names and numbers crossed out and replaced. The sheets were clearly copies and not the originals, but they were legible.

"Wow."

She flipped to the last page and scanned it. On the second to the last page she found Katharine's name. The line above it connected to Phyllis McGuinness, and Nancy followed the connections back to old Mrs. Clymer. This was a gold mine.

She looked up at him. He was smiling expectantly.

"Like I said, you may be on to something. If you

are, I don't have a clue what it means, but I have to admit I'm curious too."

"But what should I do with it?" she asked.

He shrugged. "Talk to some of the people in the chain. Like you already have been."

"But if you're curious too, why don't you do it? I mean, if someone really is a—what did you call them, intercessor?—you would know better than I would."

"A couple of reasons." He reached into his pocket for a wallet. "One, you're the one that made the connections, if there really are any. Here at the café, you probably hear more stories than I do. Second, I don't want to seem like I'm interrogating my own congregation members about their role in the chain. It might make them self-conscious, guilty, whatever. I do believe that our prayers do a lot of good, and I don't want to interfere with that."

"But it's okay if I do."

He chuckled. "No offense, but you won't have the same effect on them."

"Yeah, I guess I can see that."

He stood and put a couple of dollars on the table. Nancy quickly stood too.

"No, it's on the house."

"All right. Okay if I tip the waitress?"

The room had filled, and it occurred to her that Sally was frazzled, trying to keep up with the customers.

"Sure. Thanks. Thanks for everything."

He paused as he opened the door, and touched a finger to the brim of an imaginary hat. Then he was gone.

***

Bruce pulled into the garage at 5:45. He stuck his head in the family room and was confronted by a scene of chaos. Maddie was playing some kind of computer game, Sam and Indigo were watching TV, and Jake was arranging a string of toy cars on the coffee table. The carpet was strewn with Lego blocks, cars, dolls, pieces from board games, shoes, and scraps of paper.

Only Jake looked up. "Hi, Dad."

"Hi kids. Have you seen Mom?"

"No, not yet," Maddie said, her eyes still on the computer screen. She had a key, and they were allowed to leave the sitter's house at 5:00 to wait for Nancy or Bruce to get home.

"What have you got going there?" Bruce asked Jake.

"I put them so the fastest ones are in front and the slowest ones are in back."

Bruce squatted so he could get a better look at the cars. A Corvette led the pack, and a garbage truck brought up the rear. There were probably a few Bruce would have questioned—a Model T in the middle, for instance—but overall his son had done a pretty good job for a six year old. He gave Jake's shoulder a gentle squeeze and went upstairs.

The house was a mess. Breakfast dishes were stacked in the sink, the newspaper was lying in pieces on the table, and stacks of laundry were piled on the furniture, waiting to be sorted and folded. Bruce sighed and poured himself a glass of white wine. He retreated to the relative calm of their bedroom and slowly changed his clothes.

Flip Flaskerud, one of his loan officers, had accused him today of being stingy and uncaring. *I'm just* being a businessman, Bruce had replied, but now the words seemed like a flimsy defense. The two of them had met in Bruce's office with Ted Hanning, one of their commercial loan accounts. Hanning owned a string of car wash operations—mostly coin-operated, but a few full-service—and his business was about to go under. Spring and early summer usually brought a bonanza to the car wash industry: a continually repeating cycle of showers followed by days of glorious weather, when people would want to cruise and drop the tops of their convertibles. And the switch to daylight savings time meant that conscientious car owners could really <u>see</u> the dirt.

The problem that Hanning faced wasn't that cars weren't getting dirty--a more typical concern as Oregon headed into its three-month dry season. The problem was that with the almost constant rain, the cars were getting dirty too often and never stayed clean. People had just given up feeding quarters into the coin machines or forking over five bucks for the machine wash, and had resigned themselves to rain spots and a layer of road grime.

Flaskerud had wanted to extend Hanning's line of credit to get him through the tough spot, but Bruce had been more cautious. What if it keeps right on raining through October? What if his debt keeps piling up? The loan payments were already eating into most of the net revenue. Bruce had, though, agreed to a meeting where they could hash it out.

He had listened as sympathetically as he could to Hanning's tale of woe. He even offered to initiate the paperwork for a separate loan to cover short-term operating expenses—at a higher interest rate, of course, in view of the increased risk. Flaskerud took Hanning's side, even though it was clear that few of the assumptions in his business plan were holding true. In the end, Hanning reluctantly agreed to the new loan, and shuffled out of the meeting with his shoulders drooping.

Flaskerud stayed back, and as soon as the door was closed, lit into him.

"What was all that about? We're floating in cash we don't know what to do with—we're already getting an eight point spread on his line of credit. How can we justify gouging him for more?"

"Like I told Hanning, we're facing higher exposure on this one." Bruce said, trying to be patient.

"But we're in first position on this! Worse comes to worst, we own a bunch of car washes. They're still worth a lot more than his outstanding loan."

"Maybe. But we don't know that for sure. We're a bank, we're not in the car wash business."

"And your questions about the DEQ inspections—what's with that?"

"Settle down, Flip. They were just questions." The Oregon Department of Environmental Quality required car washes to filter and re-use their water, to conserve both water and energy. Hanning had had to retrofit several of his operations, and the equipment was expensive, accounting for at least a fifth of his loan.

Flaskerud stared at him for a moment. "Know what I think? I think you were hinting that he should sell the equipment. Since he wasn't getting inspected, no one would know that he was just dumping his water down the drain."

"Well, that would be an option for him. It would certainly help his profitability."

"But it's flat illegal!"

"Which is why I didn't tell him to do it."

Flaskerud had just shaken his head.

Bruce now replayed the conversation to himself as he went back to the kitchen. Just because he was the most productive loan officer at the branch, Flaskerud didn't have the right to lecture his boss on how the customers should be treated. No employee was so valuable that his job was guaranteed.

He looked into the refrigerator to see if there were any leftovers that he could stick in the microwave. It was almost empty. He slowly started putting the dirty dishes in the dishwasher. When he thought about it rationally, Bruce really didn't blame Nancy for the disaster the house was in. She had a full time job, just like him, so the burden had to fall on them equally. But if she was going to spend her days outside the home, she should at least be bringing in enough money to hire a housecleaning service to clean up this mess. She should be making enough money so they could go out to dinner when they wanted to instead of eating a constant series of TV dinners and thrown together, hectic meals.

A noise in the hallway interrupted his thoughts. Indigo and Sam burst into the kitchen, yelling at each other about something. A fight over the TV remote control, or something equally meaningless.

"Hey, you two." Bruce snapped at them. "Quiet down, and sort it out yourselves. I can't deal with it."

They retreated back to the family room, jabbing each other in the ribs and shouting. Bruce picked up the phone and punched in the number for the café. It was busy. He went back to the dishes and stewed.

He tried calling again a few minutes later. The line was still busy. It's not like it's the kind of place to take reservations, he thought. And they had a second line for the credit card machine.

Finally he heard the garage door, and Nancy came in carrying a bag of groceries.

"Sorry I'm late," she said. "How was your day?"

"Fine," he said, not looking at her.

"I got a U-bake lasagna for dinner," she said. "It'll only take a few minutes."

"I called to see if you wanted me to go pick something up," he said. "How come the line was always busy?"

She paused as she put a gallon of milk into the refrigerator. "I had to make a few calls."

"At this time of night? Who would be open?"

She closed the refrigerator door. "Were the kids already here when you got home?"

"Yeah. Indigo and Sam were fighting over a TV show. The usual mayhem."

"If you want to set the table, I'll take care of the rest of the dishes after dinner."

He threw place mats onto the dining room table. Another fight broke out in the family room and Nancy yelled at the kids. A squall drove fat raindrops against the sliding door, pounding out a drum roll on the glass. Bruce stared out the window at the dark cloud and tried in vain to ease the knots that had formed in his shoulders and neck.

8

"Hey Nancy! Look what the cat dragged in!"

Mary called her from out in the main room, where she had been wiping off the tables. Nancy left the desk in the kitchen to see.

"Jaime! Good to see you, you poor thing."

He grinned and limped in on a pair of crutches. Out on the street, an old sedan pulled away from the curb—probably his mother's, Nancy thought.

"It's not so bad," he said. "Look at this!" He held the crutches out at his sides and hobbled across the floor on his walking cast.

"Pretty good, huh?"

Mary and Nancy both applauded. He was wearing khaki shorts and a bright Hawaiian print shirt. Nancy walked over and took a closer look at his cast.

Jaime proudly held his left leg out, balancing the heel of the cast on the floor. "My fan club," he said.

Words were scrawled across the cast. Get better soon...A hunk with a hunk of plaster...I miss you–your dancing partner...Hey baby, you need to work on your tan...I see you are too sexy for your legs... A few of the inscriptions were in Spanish. Nancy laughed. Most of the writing was on the top and inside of the cast, mostly with the same felt pen and—it seemed—in the same handwriting.

It was only then that she noticed the remains of a

nasty bruise just below his left eye.

"Here, sit down," she said, pulling a chair out for him. "How do you feel?"

"Good." He sat down and rested the crutches against the table. "Really, I'm okay. And I never knew one of these would be such a babe magnet." He nodded toward the cast. "I should have put one on sooner."

"But you have a bruise by your eye," Mary said, leaning for a closer look.

"Aw, you're like my mother. It's almost all better." He touched it, tentatively. "I did have a headache for a while, but that's gone too." He looked at Nancy. "And I'm ready to work as much overtime as you need, boss. I gotta get some money to buy some new wheels. I miss my truck."

She laughed. "We'll see. We still haven't been very busy, and you still need to take it easy. Maybe you'll get better tips, out of sympathy."

A pair of big men wearing plaid shirts and suspenders came in and took one of the small tables near the window.

"Got to get to work," Jaime said, and pushed himself onto his feet. Nancy watched as he took their order. They both asked for lattes, and Jaime hobbled over to the espresso machine with surprising grace. Nancy shook her head and went back to the kitchen.

The sheets of paper were scattered over the small table, beckoning her like a treasure map. She sat down and leafed through them again, trying to figure out what to do with the names and numbers. Her first thought had been to find out who had called Katharine with the prayer request for Andy Brandon. She guessed it would have been someone on the same level of the chain as Phyllis

McGuinness, but there were over twenty of them. She had made some calls yesterday afternoon, but few people were home, and the ones she had been able to reach weren't much help. Besides, Mrs. Clymer had said that she sometimes recruited substitute callers from the congregation, so the person she was looking for might not even be on the list.

She sighed and put the sheets into a folder. Another stack of paper confronted her: bills for supplies, utilities, and the loan payment for the business. She added the numbers on a calculator and then dug out the receipt for yesterday's cash deposit. The bank account balance was slightly higher than the amount of the bills, but that meant the only way she was going to cover her payroll checks in a week was through whatever they took in between now and then. Even in a good week it would be difficult.

She looked through her bills to see which ones she could put off. The wholesale food supplier never cut her much slack, and she needed to keep her account to get the discounts. The electricity and gas utilities were big and bureaucratic, and wouldn't hesitate to shut her off for non-payment. The city's water bill was another matter. She was already a month behind, but she knew they would call her before shutting the water off, so it was worth taking a chance.

She put the rest of the bills in a large envelope; she would write the checks in the evening when she had more time.

***

Bruce and the kids watched a Disney video while Nancy sat at her desk in the corner of the family room. She paid the bills by hand, filing the invoices in a folder labeled "Paid Bills." Bruce had urged her to put her accounts and bill payments on the computer, and she knew he was right. Gathering the paperwork to complete her taxes had been a nightmare. But she did some of the accounting at the restaurant when she had a spare moment, and didn't want the headache of two computers. Besides, the time to make the conversion was at the beginning of the year, so she could put it off for another few months.

The phone rang and Nancy picked it up.

"Hello, Nan?" It was a woman's voice.

Nancy had a hard time hearing over the movie soundtrack, so she carried the phone into the hall.

"Sorry, I couldn't hear you. Who are you calling for?"

"Nan. Nan Johnson. I have a prayer request."

"Maybe you have the wrong number. This is 333-6019."

"Oh! I'm sorry! I thought I dialed 333-6109. Sorry to bother you."

Nancy started to push the "End" button on the phone, then caught herself.

"Wait! Are you still there?"

There was a pause. "Yes?"

"You said you had a prayer request for, uh, Nan."

"That's right."

"Are you a member of the Cedar Creek Community Church, by any chance?"

"Yes, I am. Why?"

Nancy felt goosebumps on her arms. "Well, my

name is Nancy Mackay, and I was talking to Pastor Montgomery about your church's prayer chain. Can I ask where you are in the chain?"

"What do you mean?"

"Do the people you call talk to anyone else, or are they at the end of the chain?"

"They're at the end, I suppose. There's nothing stopping them from passing the prayer request on to a friend, I guess, but I know they are not assigned anyone to call. Are you a member of our church, Nancy? I don't remember meeting you."

"No, afraid not. I own the Fir Away Café in town. A friend of mine, Katharine Regan, is a member of the church, and she's the one that got me interested in the prayer chain."

"Oh, yes, I know Katharine. I called her a few weeks ago."

Nancy's pulse quickened. "She's not on your regular call list?"

"No, I was covering for someone else."

This was too much to hope for. "Was the call, by any chance, about Andy Brandon's kidney stone?"

There was silence on the line. Had she pushed too far? Nancy was a complete stranger, after all. And so was the person on the other line—if she hung up now, Nancy wouldn't even have her name.

"Hello? Are you still there?"

"Oh, yes. I was just trying to remember. I really don't know. I do remember that prayer request, but I can't say that is what I called Katharine about. Why do you want to know?"

"Uh, Andy Brandon was in my restaurant when he had his kidney stone attack. I was just curious. Say, do you mind if I ask your name?"

"Not at all. My name is Stephanie Ong."

"Well, thanks Stephanie. I'm afraid I've interrupted your evening duties."

"It's okay. I'm the one that dialed the wrong number."

"Well, to make it worth your while, I'd be glad to pray for whoever is on your list tonight, if you like."

"Hmm. I don't see any harm in that. The prayer request is for Flip Flaskerud, whose father passed away."

"Okay. I will add a prayer for him."

"Thank you. Well, goodnight, uh, Nancy."

"Goodnight, Stephanie."

God forgive me, Nancy thought as she rushed to her desk to scribble a page of notes from the conversation. It was the closest she could come to a prayer.

***

They sipped glasses of white wine in the hot tub and listened to the drizzle gently tap the roof. Nancy was lost in her own thoughts, worrying about the business and wondering how she could turn it around. Bruce had his eyes closed.

After a while she said, "You didn't mention that Flip's dad died." He had been in hospice care for cancer for the past three months and Bruce had told her about the toll it was taking on Flip.

Bruce opened his eyes. "He didn't. What makes you think he did?"

Nancy sat up and looked at him. "Are you sure? The call I got while you were watching the movie—it was a wrong number. They were calling someone to pray for

Flip Flaskerud, because his father had just passed away."

"Maybe they were talking about someone else."

"Come on. There can't be more than one Flip Flaskerud in the whole Portland area."

"Yeah, I suppose so. Well, I saw Flip a few times today and he never said anything about it."

Nancy started to climb out of the tub.

"Where are you going?" Bruce asked.

"I've got to call her. I have to stop them."

"Hold on." He grabbed her arm. "It's eleven o'clock. You're not calling anyone at this time of night."

"You don't understand."

"No kidding. What do you mean, you have to stop them?"

Nancy slid back into the hot tub. "It's a long story."

"Oh?"

She began at the beginning, telling him about the prayer chain and its connection with Karen Smith's affair with Dave Kendall, Mary Mowatt's divorce, Andy Brandon's kidney stone, and Jaime Saldivar's car accident.

"Those aren't the only strange things happening, either," she said. "Remember when I told you that Shirley Collins almost had her kidney removed by mistake? And the weird behavior of some of the customers at the bank?"

"You don't say." The drizzle turned to a harder rain that drummed against the plastic roof and sizzled on the deck around them. "Hey, maybe it even accounts for the weather," Bruce said. "You know, someone put out a prayer request for Wayne. Get it? Wayne, rain." He chortled, then started making a sound like the beginning of the Twighlight Zone.

Nancy turned away from him. *I knew I shouldn't have told him.*

They didn't speak for a few minutes.

"You seriously think there's something to this?" Bruce finally asked, quietly.

"Yes."

"Oh." He scooted higher in the tub to cool down. His hair was damp from the steam and humid air and hung over his forehead. "I mean, how could those things really be happening? It doesn't make any sense."

"I know it doesn't make sense. But I just think there are too many connections for it to be coincidence."

Bruce tilted his head, thinking about it. "Still seems too weird to be true."

***

Maddie joined her mother at the café the next day. She put the chairs upside down on the tables and swept the floor, then took a rag and some bleach and wiped the tabletops. She whistled a song and occasionally paused to look out the window at the passing traffic. Nancy kept an eye on her from the kitchen, checking herself from saying anything when Maddie missed a spot.

"Uh oh. It looks like I'm being replaced." Jaime came swinging in on his crutches.

Maddie smiled shyly. "I'm just helping Mom. She isn't paying me. Well, not much. She said she would give me my allowance if I worked here today."

"Sounds like extortion to me."

Maddie grinned and shrugged. Nancy knew she didn't have an idea what Jaime was talking about.

"How's the leg, Jaime?" Nancy called out through

the pass-through window.

"Just fine. A little itchy, though. When I took Serena to the movies last night, she wanted me to park in the handicapped spot. Can you believe that? Me, handicapped?"

"What movie did you see?"

"Huh?"

"Last night. What did you see?"

"Oh. Some chick flick. Don't even remember the name. Serena chose it." He leaned his crutches against the counter and picked up a stack of paper place mats.

Maddie watched him. "You look like a leopard," she said.

"You like my shirt, huh? All the girls go for it."

She giggled.

Nancy said, "Maddie, honey, if you're done with the tables, you can help Mary fix the soup."

"Why, is it broken?" She laughed at her joke and glanced at Jaime.

"Good one," he said, and winked at her.

"She's only nine, Jaime," Nancy said.

When the noon rush came, Maddie helped bus the tables, and carried out glasses and pitchers of ice water. Nancy had just taken an order for a cheese, lettuce, tomato and sprouts sandwich grilled on dark rye when the phone rang.

"It's for you, Nancy," Mary called from the kitchen.

"Hello?"

"Hey. It's me." Bruce's voice sounded strained.

"Hi sweetie. What's up?"

The line was quiet for a moment. "Flip just left for the nursing home. He got a call…his father died. About a half hour ago."

"Oh, that's too bad." She knew she should be sympathetic, but all she could think was, *I told you so.*

"Nancy, what's happening? The call you got last night—are you sure she said that he had already died? Couldn't she have said that they were praying because he *was* dying, or something like that?"

"No. I'm sure about what she said."

"Oh, man. It's giving me the creeps. Maybe I should have let you stop them, like you wanted to."

"It's not your fault, hon. Besides, I'm not sure it would have done any good. He's been sick for a while, hasn't he? You said he could go any time."

"I guess. Still."

"Listen, I've got to get back to work here. Don't be too late coming home tonight. Maybe we can take a walk or something."

"Yeah. That would be good."

Nancy put down the phone and thought for a minute. With the call the night before, she had enough information to get to the bottom of the prayer chain. Assuming, though, that the pastor had been right about his guess that someone had some unique power. An intercessor, he had called them.

She shivered slightly and picked up two plates that Mary had pushed across the serving counter. It would have to wait.

***

During the mid-afternoon lull, Nancy drove Maddie to Sarah's house to join the other children, then returned to the café. She pulled a folded piece of paper from her back jeans pocket—her notes from last night's conversation—and sat down at the small desk in the kitchen. She found Stefanie Ong's name near the bottom of the stack of pages that Pastor Montgomery had given her. Underneath it was typed the names and phone numbers of two people—Nan Johnson and Bernice Burns. A third—Walt Tobie—had been hand-written below the other two. The typed phone number for Bernice Burns had been crossed out and replaced with a handwritten number. She had apparently been part of the prayer chain for a while—long enough, anyway, to have lived in two homes.

She started calling the numbers, in the order they appeared on the sheet. Nan Johnson didn't answer, and didn't even seem to have an answering machine. She called the second number and let it ring five times. She was about to push the flash button when a reedy voice said, "Hello, Burns residence."

"Is this Bernice Burns?" Nancy asked.

"Certainly. What can I do for you, miss?"

Nancy paused. She had enough experience with cold calls, but this one was different. What kind of question did one use to smoke out an intercessor?

"I'm, uh, calling about the prayer chain. The one with the Cedar Creek Community Church."

"Do we have a new prayer request? And do you eventually intend to reveal your name?" The voice sounded intelligent, and Nancy could hear the faint clicking of dentures.

"Oh! Sorry. My name is Nancy Mackay. No, I don't have a prayer request. I'm just curious about something. You see, I talked to Stephanie Ong last night, and she said she was calling you as part of the prayer chain. She said the prayer request was for Flip Flaskerud, because his father had died. Do you remember that?"

"Of course. Is that what you're curious about—my memory? It is as good as ever, although I wish I could say the same about some of my other faculties. So, Miss Mackay, what kind of job do you do that requires you to survey old peoples' memories?"

"No, it isn't a job. It's, uh, a personal thing. And what I'm really curious about it this: have you noticed that your prayers often come true?"

"Why, of course they do. That's why we pray, after all. Don't you think so?"

"I don't know. I mean, if that was always true, we could just pray to end world hunger and wars, or to eliminate disease."

"Ah, but those aren't specific enough. I admit I have tried praying that kind of prayer, but either I did it wrong, or God had other plans. He can be that way sometimes, you know."

"But when you pray a more specific prayer, like for an individual person, it often comes true?"

"Why yes. Of course, I leave miracles to others. I would not pray, for instance, for an accident victim who had died to come back to life, or for a woman who had had a hysterectomy to conceive a child. In the past I've tried those, too, but have only been frustrated or saddened when they did not come to pass."

"Uh huh. But Miss Burns, have—"

"It's missus. I am—or was—married. And I don't care much for this miz thing that people use, although I can see the efficiency in it."

"Okay. Mrs. Burns, has anything bad ever happened because of one of your prayers?"

"Heavens no! Why would anyone pray for a <u>bad</u> thing to happen?"

"Well, maybe not intentionally, but, you know, by accident."

"Hmph."

"Alright, here's an example. You prayed last night for Flip Flaskerud because his father died. But Flip works for my husband, and I know that his father didn't die yesterday. In fact, he didn't die until just a couple of hours ago."

"Oh my!" Nancy could hear a TV in the background. Probably a Matlock rerun. "Are you certain of this?"

"Yes. My husband called me around noon to say that Flip had left for the nursing home because his father had just passed away."

"Well. I knew that Flip had been struggling with his father's illness, the poor dear. He had been quite sick, you know. And are you saying that our prayers somehow hastened his demise?"

"I don't know. I suppose it could be coincidence. Are you sure you haven't noticed anything else like this happening? Where you pray maybe for the wrong thing, and it comes true even though it shouldn't have?"

"Now really, Miss Mackay, why would I pray for the wrong thing?"

"Oh, I know you wouldn't, knowingly. But the prayer chain has a lot of links. The message can get garbled. Like last night, when the chain was saying that Mr. Flaskerud had died."

"Well. I still don't see it. We were praying for the young Flaskerud, Flip. I certainly wasn't praying that his father would pass on, even though the information I received was, as you say, misleading."

A customer came into the café. "Okay. Well, I appreciate your taking the time to talk to me. If I give you my number, could you call me if you notice any strange patterns to your prayer requests?"

"Yes, I would be glad to," she said.

***

Bruce had to work late that night, after all. Nancy fed the children a dinner of spaghetti with sauce from a jar, and cherry Jell-O.

"Hey Mom, do you want to shoot some hoops with me?" Sam asked when they were done eating.

She looked out the window, checking to see if there was a break in the rain. "Okay, if you'll help me with the dishes."

He brought the plates into the kitchen, and started on the cups, but drifted off when he heard laughter in the family room. Nancy shook her head and finished cleaning up.

She had written down the names and phone numbers of the last two people in the prayer chain, and brought them home from work. Her first call was to Nan Johnson, who admitted to being a long-time member of the prayer chain, but also confessed that she often ran out of time and wasn't able to do the prayers like she was supposed to. The children were making so much noise it was hard for Nancy to hear what she was saying. She realized, after she put down the phone, that the noise had come from the other end of the line.

Walt Tobie was home, too. He was eager to talk about the prayer chain and readily agreed that the prayers could be coming true, "at least in a general way." But he had only been part of the chain for a couple of weeks.

Sam was perched on the arm of a couch, watching TV. "Come on, I'll shoot some baskets with you," Nancy said.

He sprang up, and was immediately joined by Jake and Indigo. They played horse at the hoop over the street in front of their house, jumping out of the way when the ball hit a puddle. Sam tried a backward shot over his head, and by some miracle it went in. When Indigo's turn came she faced away from the basket, leaned back, and heaved. The wet ball slipped from her fingers and bounced off her forehead, almost knocking her off her feet. Nancy held her breath, waiting for her daughter's reaction. Jake and Sam bent over in laughter and Indigo started giggling, crossing her eyes and spinning around in the street like a cartoon character.

Bruce pulled up when the game was nearly over, and joined in for the last few shots. It started sprinkling and they all went in.

The kids drifted toward the family room and Bruce pulled Nancy aside.

"You've got to stop it," he said.

"What?"

"This prayer chain thing. You were right last night when you said you had to stop it."

She didn't know what to say. He mistook her hesitance.

"It's crazy," he hissed. "It's just like they killed Flip's father, for no good reason."

"Well, in the first place, we can't be sure that's what happened. He might have died anyway. And besides, it isn't mine to stop. The church runs it, and I'm sure I wouldn't have any influence over them."

"Yeah, they made it happen, all right. There are too many coincidences—you said so yourself. That guy with the kidney stone, Mary's husband going goofy on her, and all the rest. There are—"

"But even if it's true, nothing bad really happened in the end. Things turned out all right."

"Sure, tell that to Flip Flaskerud. And Mary would have killed herself if John hadn't found her. And that woman who almost had the wrong operation—what if they hadn't caught it in time? And Jaime's car crash— what if he had broken his neck instead of his leg?"

"But he didn't! That's my point. Maybe there is…something…that keeps things from really going bad. I'm not so sure I'm supposed to interfere with it."

He stared at her. "Do you really believe that? Do you think God or some angel is watching over all this stuff and only letting it go so far?"

She shrugged.

"That's nuts," he said, and looked away.

Nancy bit her lip.

"You could talk to that minister," Bruce said, looking back at her. "What was his name?"

"Montgomery. Dave Montgomery."

"Yeah. Talk to him. Tell them to stop it. It may be harmless to you, but I was with Flip when he got the phone call today. Losing his father hit him really hard."

"But he had been sick for months. It was only a matter of time," she said quietly.

"That's easy for you to say. There was always a hope, and Flip held on to it. Now that's gone too."

Through the dining room window, Nancy watched the setting sun send its light through a hole in the clouds.

Rays spread out from west to east, turning the bottom of the clouds a reddish gold.

"All right," she said. "I'll talk to him."

9

"Want some coffee? I'm afraid it's from Costco, but it's all we can afford."

"Sure. And I'll let you in on a little secret: I buy my beans from Costco too."

The young pastor disappeared into the church's kitchen. Nancy took the opportunity to survey his office. Like a lawyer, he had shelves crammed with books. C.S. Lewis, Bonhofer, Thomas à Kempis. One of the shelves was devoted to topics: well-thumbed volumes on marriage, raising children, money, grief, divorce, retirement. Another held a variety of Bibles (why does he need more than one?) and some thick reference books.

His desk was relatively neat. The obligatory family portraits were missing, replaced instead by a couple of framed copies of cartoons. A notebook computer was pushed to a corner, with a loose stack of papers on the keyboard and a collection of post-it notes stuck around the screen.

A framed copy of a poem about footprints in the sand was hung on the wall, along with a poster of Bart Simpson writing on a blackboard. "Body parts are not for hanging donuts," it said. In front of her on the small conference table was a brightly colored plastic Bart Simpson statue with its arm in the air. She pulled down on the arm.

"Cowabunga, man," the statue said. A peanut M&M rolled out of a hole in the toe of the plastic shoe. The church secretary in the adjoining office glanced up briefly and smiled. Nancy gave her an embarrassed shrug and ate the M&M.

"Here you go," the pastor said, and slid a mug in front of her as he sat down.

"This somehow seems out of place," she nodded toward the dispenser.

"What? Having candy in the office?"

"No. The Simpsons theme. I won't even let my kids watch it"

"Ah. Well, it does cause some consternation for some of the members of my flock. But really, the show does treat religion fairly gently. And at least it talks about it. Did you see the episode where Homer becomes a missionary? Or the one where Bart becomes a faith healer?"

She shrugged and shook her head.

"Pity." He took a sip of his coffee. "So how's your investigation of our prayer chain coming?"

"I'm not sure. Bruce wanted me to ask you to put an end to it."

He raised his eyebrows. "Bruce?"

"Sorry. My husband."

"Ah. And why does he feel that way?"

A better question would be, why doesn't he come in and talk about it himself, Nancy thought.

"One of the people he works with is Flip Flaskerud. His father just died, but it wasn't until after the prayer chain had a message about him dying."

"How do you know that?"

Nancy told him about phone call from Stephanie

Ong that she had intercepted.

"And you think that the prayer actually caused the man to die?" he asked.

"I don't know. It seems like the pattern has happened too often just to be a coincidence. Of all people, you should be able to accept that possibility."

"Why? Because of my faith?"

She nodded.

He picked up a loose pen from the table and turned it in his hands. "I suppose you're right. Have you heard of the studies that have been done on the power of prayer in healing?"

"Maybe," she said. "I saw a TV show once where there seemed to be scientific evidence supporting it. People in hospitals were more likely to get well when there were people praying for them."

"Exactly."

"But here's something that was strange about it. People didn't need to be near the people they were praying for, and they didn't even have to know them personally. Okay, I can accept that. But it didn't even seem to matter which god people were praying to, or whether they were praying to a god at all. How do you reconcile that?"

"Hmm. Good question. What do you think?"

"Don't ask me. I'm not the one who went to seminary."

He chuckled and waited a moment for her to speak. She didn't.

"Well, here's an idea," he said. "God wants us to pray about things; in fact, he commands us to. So maybe when we actually do, he's pleased enough about it to actually intervene for us, whether or not we acknowledge that he is the one doing the work. I don't know, though. You'll have to ask him yourself some day."

Nancy felt a little uncomfortable and squirmed in her chair.

"So. Can you stop it?" she asked.

"The prayer chain? I don't know. It would be hard, and I'm not convinced I should. Besides, the main problem isn't that folks are praying, it's that the message is getting garbled, right?"

"Well, yes."

"So maybe there's a way to fix that."

He rested his hand on his chin.

"Want another?" he asked.

"What?"

He tilted his head toward the little Bart.

"Oh!" She felt herself blush. "Okay."

She pulled down on Bart's arm.

"Eat my shorts!" Another M&M rolled out. A blue one this time.

"What if you sent out the prayer requests through an e-mail message, or by fax?" she asked, chewing on the M&M.

"I don't know. I thought about it, but we couldn't afford to issue everyone fax machines. And a lot of the folks would be lost with e-mail." He looked at the ceiling and laughed.

"What?"

"I was picturing some of the congregation members—like old Mac O'Connor, or Betty Scruggs—getting tangled up in a mouse cord, or cussing at Microsoft Windows. I wouldn't be surprised if some of them still have rotary phones."

"Hmm." They were silent for a while. Nancy

heard the crunch of a stapler as the secretary organized some papers. She looked at her watch and realized she needed to be at work.

"What if you reorganized the chain?" she asked. "You know, put the people who mix up the message at the bottom, so they aren't calling anyone?"

"Do you know who those people are?"

She shrugged. "Not exactly. Someone above Stephanie Ong, probably. I would guess it would be older people, who can't hear very well."

He nodded. "And that would be a problem. It would seem sort of discriminatory if we put them at the bottom of the chain. And besides, they really like making the calls—sort of a legitimate form of gossip. It would take most of the fun out of it if all they could do was pray."

"I didn't know the point was about having fun."

"Of course it isn't, but you know what I mean. For a lot of the retired folks, it's the highlight of their day. Like getting mail."

She sighed. "Well, I have to get to work. Let me know if you think of anything." She stood to leave.

"Sure." He stood, too. "Say, is your restaurant open on Sundays?"

"Yes. I would rather not have to keep it open then, but we would lose too much business from the skiers and tourists passing through. Why?"

"Do you work then? Don't you take any time off?"

"Oh. No, I usually leave it up to the weekend chef and a few waitresses."

"Well, then. We'd be glad to have you pay us a visit. In the summer our services start at nine and ten thirty…"

"Okay," she said, tentatively. "I'll think about it."

***

"There you are!" Mary was leaning against the front of the building, trying to stay out of the rain.

"What's the matter? Don't you have your key?"

"No. Look." She gestured toward the lock. A padlock had been hooked just below the door latch, preventing it from opening.

"What the…" Nancy leaned in for a closer look. An official-looking form had been taped to the door next to the padlock.

> These premises have been secured against entry by order of the Comptroller of the First Federated Bank of the Cascades. For inquiries, please contact the Division Manager, Overdue Accounts Section, at (503)425-5415.

Nancy stared at the form. How could they have done this? Her loan payment was late again, but they had always cut her some slack in the past.

A car pulled into one of the parking spaces on the street, then slowly moved back into traffic. Nancy couldn't see who was in it, but they had obviously decided the café was closed.

She collapsed onto the welcome mat and held her head in her hands. The rain felt warm on her cheeks, and she realized that it wasn't rain.

"It'll be okay," Mary said helpfully.

"Yeah," Nancy whispered. What was Bruce going to say? Where was she going to get the money to make the loan payment? Cars drove by on the rain-slicked pavement, indifferent to her problems.

"Hey, what's up?"

Nancy reluctantly raised her head and looked. "Hi Isaac. The bank locked us out."

"You're kidding. They can't do that!"

"Well, they did."

"They put a sign on the door," Mary said.

Isaac lifted the brim of his hat and bent to read it. "Well I'll be." He straightened, pulling a kink out of his back. "Don't you have a key to the back door?"

"Yeah, I suppose. But it goes through the storeroom and kitchen. I can't have customers walking through there."

"Come on," he said, holding out his hand. He pulled Nancy to her feet.

The cafe was part of a row of old buildings—some had common walls, and the others were built within inches of each other. To get to the back they had to walk past four storefronts to a driveway that took them to a narrow potholed alley. The rain had picked up and none of them had an umbrella. They huddled against an east wind and jumped over puddles. Nancy searched in her purse for a key and opened the lock. The wood door had expanded in its frame, and she had to use her shoulder to get it to budge. They stood on a battered wood floor and shook the water off their arms and heads. Mary laughed. "We look like dogs," she said.

Nancy squeezed through boxes stacked in the

small back porch and opened the door into the kitchen. She groped for the light switch and was greeted by the familiar sight of pots hanging on the walls and the massive steel griddle that dominated the room. At least the bank hadn't gotten in here and hauled it all away.

Isaac slipped past her into the main room. "Okay. Where's a screwdriver?" he called.

"What do you have in mind?" Nancy asked through the pass-through window.

"Phillips, it looks like."

"No, I mean, what are you going to do?"

"You'll see."

Nancy rummaged in a drawer full of small tools, and took the screwdriver to him.

"Should I fire up the grill?" Mary asked.

"No, don't bother," Nancy said.

"Yes! Do it, Mary," Isaac said. The screws were covered with a half dozen layers of paint, and he struggled to break the first one loose. Nancy stood back and watched, immobilized by despair.

"Ta da!" Isaac pulled the handle off the door, and outside the latch hit the ground with a clatter. He opened the door and retrieved it. "The Fir Away Cafe is now open for business."

"It won't do any good," Nancy said.

"All right. I'll buy two cups of coffee instead of one. At your markup, that ought to keep you out of debtors prison for at least another month."

Nancy gave a weak laugh. "The bank will just board it up again. See, I just don't have any money left to pay them." She spoke quietly so Mary wouldn't hear. She knew her cook would offer up her paycheck without hesitation, even though she really couldn't afford to.

Lacking a latch, the door gently blew open. Isaac pushed it shut with his foot and inspected the padlock that he was holding. "I bet I can get the old guy at Fritzie Welding to saw this thing off." He looked up at Nancy. "Now you just go down there and reason with those people. Don't they understand you'll never pay off your loan if you can't make any money? Oh, and before you go, I still need my coffee."

Nancy went through the motions of filling the pot and sliding in a fresh filter full of ground coffee. "I don't know. Bruce and I plowed a lot of our own money into this place. I'm sure the bank knows they can repossess it now and get most of the loan back. The longer they wait, the farther into the hole I go."

"Yeah, and speaking of Bruce, didn't you get the loan through his bank? Why can't he get them off your back?"

"No. Fact is, it's worse with him working there. He's management—it makes him look bad. I'm almost afraid to go home tonight."

"Ah. He won't hit you, now will he?"

"No, no. Nothing like that. But he'll be mad. Maybe not at me, but he'll still be cranky." Steaming black coffee began filling the carafe.

There was a thump on the door. A brown eye peeked through the hole where the lock had been.

"Hey there! What happened to the handle?"

"Ah jes pulled out mah 38 and shot it off." Isaac moved his foot and said, "Come on in, sir."

"Que pasa?" Jaime said, slipping through. He was wearing a T-shirt made to look like a cheesy tuxedo, and baggy denim shorts.

"Just a problem with the thingamajig," Isaac said,

holding it so he couldn't see the padlock. "I'm running it down to the shop, as soon as the coffee is ready."

Nancy felt a sudden urge to move, to get out of the restaurant. "Can you two hold down the fort for a while?" she asked.

"No problem," Mary called from the kitchen. Jaime nodded. With so few customers, they would probably be bored if she stayed, Nancy thought.

"Thanks, Isaac," she said.

"Sure. So are you going to do what I told you?"

"I don't know. I'll try."

***

The house was empty. The kids were still at Sarah's, and with luck they hadn't seen her car drive past. She crawled into the storage space under the basement stairs and turned on a flashlight, illuminating a beam of dust particles. She rested the light on the floor, and started moving Easter baskets, Christmas decorations, spare suitcases, boxes of old tax returns, and several pairs of baby shoes. After she had cleared an aisle, she slid out a heavy box that was sealed with yellowing packing tape. She pushed it into the hall, and bent to the task of returning everything else to its place. Bruce wouldn't miss the box, but she didn't want any questions about what she had been looking for.

She hefted the box and lugged it into the trunk of her car. She then returned to the house and began rummaging through the top drawer of her dresser, filling the bottom of a small cloth bag. Her eyes swept around the bedroom, and she forced herself to leave before anything else joined the collection.

Liquid Louie's Pawn was in a brick building in the market district, where she sometimes shopped for good produce deals. She hadn't paid much attention to it before, and only vaguely remembered its location. She parked in the front, and looked around, as if she were being followed. Black iron bars protected the windows, but she could still see the cluttered shelves loaded with guitars, brass instruments, cameras and binoculars, watches, jewelry, and portable stereo systems. She slipped her purse strap over the shoulder, and locked the door, leaving the box in the trunk. She didn't want to look that desperate.

The shop smelled of electronics, leather, and cigarettes. The latter was probably due to a short Lebanese man who sat on a stool behind the counter, reading a racing guide and smoking. He was totally uninterested in the fact that he had a potential customer.

Nancy pretended to look at a display of jewelry in a glass case. It took two minutes before he finally spoke. "Something you want?"

Nancy turned to the counter. "Actually, I'm thinking of selling something."

"What you got?" he said, having difficulty pulling his eyes away from the racing guide. His teeth were yellow from the tobacco, and it seemed the ends of his mustache whiskers were singed. A hazard of filterless cigarettes, she guessed.

"A ring." She pulled it out of the bag and put it on the counter. "It was my grandmother's. It's solid gold."

Louie—if that was his name—grunted and hefted the ring. He turned his back to her and weighed it on a small scale on his desk.

"Hundred fifty dollars."

"Is that all? There's a lot of gold in it."

"Too small to fit on most ladies' hands. Takes money to melt it down or make it bigger."

She hesitated, then pulled out another one. It was smaller, but it had a ruby. "How about this?"

He brought it to his eye, and weighed it. "Hundred twenty five."

Another two rings, three bracelets, four necklaces and a hand full of brooches and pendants came out of the bag, and as he picked up each one from her, she felt her heart grow heavier. They had been hand-me-downs or gifts for special occasions, and although she didn't wear them much, she had always assumed she would pass them on to Maddie and Indigo. She didn't haggle over the price, and didn't know if he expected her to.

"Okay?" he asked when she was done.

"Uh, not quite. I've got something in the car."

He made no attempt to help her. She struggled under the weight of the box and had to put it down to open the shop door. She bent over and pushed it across the floor to the counter.

"Do you have a knife?" It was, she realized, an absurd question. One whole shelf was devoted to various hunting knives, jack knives, and Leatherman tools.

Instead of coming around the corner, he just handed her a box knife. She cut the tape and pulled out a plate. She set it carefully on the counter.

"It's china. A full set, twelve of everything. There isn't a chip or a scratch on any of it."

"I don't deal in dishes. You need a second hand store."

"No, this is very valuable china. It would cost thousands to buy new." She really didn't have any idea what it was worth. She and Bruce had been given an 8-piece china set when they were married, but they rarely used it. She had inherited this set from her grandmother and had just kept it in storage.

He turned the plate over and inspected it. He shrugged, and gestured toward the box. She started pulling out the rest of the dishes and stacking them on the counter. He looked at the bottom of one of the plates again and then pulled over an old laptop computer that was at the back of his desk. It seemed incongruous in here, and she suspected that one of his customers had brought it in, desperate for cash. Or, just as likely, it had been lifted from the seat of a parked car.

"All right. Eight hundred dollars."

"No, it has to be worth more than that."

He shrugged and closed the lid of the laptop.

She started putting the plates back in the box, and he surprised her by saying, "Okay, a thousand, but that's as high as I can go."

***

Her next stop was the bank, not the main office where the nasty note on the door had come from, but her local branch in Cedar Creek. She knew the commercial loan officer well and would stand a better chance there.

She had over two thousand dollars in cash from Liquid Louie. She knew she should have had the jewelry and china appraised, and then sold through a dealer specializing in those items. For that matter, she could have made a lot more money through e-bay. But she didn't have the luxury of time, and she tried to convince herself not to dwell on it.

Virginia Metzler seemed to be expecting Nancy to contact her. She had a glass cubicle on the second floor of the bank branch. Nancy hadn't been in it much, and wasn't thrilled to be there now.

"Did you know they locked me out of my restaurant?" Nancy asked, skipping small talk.

"Yes, I'm afraid so. But it wasn't my decision, Nancy."

"Don't they realize it will be awfully hard to make my loan payments if I don't have any customers?"

Virginia was silent for a moment, reading—or at least pretending to—one of the documents in Nancy's file. "As far as the bank is concerned, the loan has been cancelled. Didn't you get the letter? It was sent certified."

"Yes, but I made a payment when I got the letter."

"A partial payment."

"Well, yeah."

Virginia looked up. "See, that's the problem. Your business has been late or delinquent on most of the loan payments in the last six months. I know you're working hard at making it succeed, but from a bank's perspective, it's a bad risk."

"All right. I'll get it caught up."

Virginia raised her eyebrows. "With what? Your checking account balance has been averaging near zero for a couple of months."

To Nancy it seemed like an invasion of privacy, but she couldn't blame the bank for keeping an eye on it. "I have twenty-three hundred dollars. I was going to deposit that today, and it will get me caught up."

"Really? Where did that come from?"

"We've had a good week. Things are turning around, and the place has been hopping. I should have brought it in earlier, but just didn't have the time."

Virginia was silent for a moment. "Well, you shouldn't have that much cash sitting in your register. It isn't safe."

"Yes, I know."

"It still won't leave enough to pay your other bills, will it?"

"They're mostly current. I can pay the bills that haven't come in yet out of the rest of the month's revenue. The big ones have already come in—grocery supplies, water and sewer, electricity." Most of which still sat on her desk, unpaid. She hoped the bank hadn't done too much research on her creditors.

"I don't know. What are you going to do in the fall?"

"What do you mean?"

"Summer should be your busiest time, right? With the tourists? If you can barely make ends meet now, how would you stay afloat then?"

"Well, I'm getting more and more local customers. It will keep building by word of mouth. Last winter I got quite a few skiers, too."

"Maybe, but you were still coasting on your initial financing."

"But it takes time to build a clientele. I'm sure this bank has more customers now than when it first opened. Right?"

Virginia shrugged. "I suppose." She flipped through some pages in the file. "Like I said, it isn't my decision. But I can make a few calls, and see if they'll cut you some slack."

"Thanks. I would really appreciate it."

She swiveled in her chair and typed some codes

into her computer. "I show that you are delinquent in your loan account by nineteen hundred and fifty-four dollars. Are you going to pay that now?"

"Yes."

"Do you have it with you?"

"Oh. Sure." Nancy pulled the bills out of her pocketbook. They were mostly hundreds. Not the typical currency that would be lying in the cash register of a café. She hoped Virginia wouldn't notice.

Virginia took them without comment. She counted the money and wrote out a receipt. "We should have a decision by tomorrow morning. How should I reach you?"

Just call me at the shop, Nancy was about to say, then realized that it might be best if the bank didn't know she had removed the lock. "Call me on the cell phone." She gave Virginia the number.

"You realize I can't guarantee anything?"

"Yeah. Do whatever you can, though."

10

She could hear the hallway clock strike two-thirty. Nancy stared at the ceiling, watching a changing pattern of gray and black as the light from a street light was filtered by the leaves of a maple. Bruce was asleep beside her. He hadn't been angry, as she thought he would be. He didn't say anything when he got home, even though he must have known. He waited for her to tell him, and just shook his head when she said that Isaac had helped get the lock off. Nancy had of course omitted mention of the visit to the pawnshop. He asked if she had had to dig into their savings account to get caught up on the loan payment, and she said, no, she had been able to do it by emptying the cash register and what was left in her business account. Are you sure you don't want to pack it in? he had asked her, but when she said no, he didn't push it.

But the truth was, she didn't know what she wanted to do. By this time of the year, the town should have been host to a steady stream of motor homes, campers, and trucks pulling boats, jet skis and other toys as the residents of the Willamette valley headed for the Cascade Mountains. Even though only a small fraction stopped for a meal, it was enough to make a real difference. And she knew from her own experience growing up in Portland that once a family found a place on the road they liked, they would often make a routine of stopping there to break up the trip. She remembered stopping for pastries at Heidi's on the way to Mt. Hood for skiing, or at Joe's Donuts at the little town of Sandy, or pulling in for a bowl of chili at the Huckleberry Inn in Government Camp.

She had hoped that, over time, her Fir Away Café would become one of those favorite stopping places. But she was at a loss for how to make people actually come in. Word of mouth was a huge factor in restaurants, but most of her customers were locals who wouldn't have much influence on the visitors. She had—she thought— installed an attractive sign: a painting of a fir tree next to a steaming cup of coffee that projected over the sidewalk above the front door. It was designed to convey an image of small town charm, and the fir tree was supposed to appeal to the vacationers heading for the national forests and recreation areas. But so far it didn't seem to be working. She had even tried to get the food reporter from The Oregonian to feature her restaurant in an article, but he had always had excuses that his list of pending reviews was too long, and Cedar Creek was too far away to be of interest to most of their readers.

If it was any consolation, her restaurant wasn't the only one to be hit by the dearth of tourist traffic. Steve Pitt, an ex-hippie in his late thirties with a long ponytail and an earring, owned the Snipe Hunt Pub. "Only the die hard fishermen are left," he told her, "and even they're getting scarce. The fish aren't biting, and there isn't much joy in popping open a beer when the rain is dripping down your neck." His business was down thirty percent compared to most summers, he said.

But none of this helped her current predicament. She just didn't know what to do. She could cut back on staff, but then her service would suffer, and she would lose more customers. She could close on the slowest days—typically Sunday and Monday—but that would drive away customers, too, if they couldn't count on the place being open. Increasing prices wasn't an option; she was already near the top of the comfort range for casual dining, and the locals were well aware of what her competitors charged for coffee and a meal. She could try more advertising and coupons, but that took money that she didn't have. Besides, the problem was that traffic through town had plunged, and advertising wasn't going to make the campers and hikers suddenly jump into their cars.

She thought about Dave Montgomery, and the comfort that she had felt sitting in his office. What would his advice be? He would hear her out, ask a few questions, and then gently ask her what she thought she needed to do. No advice at all, in other words. Well, not quite. He would encourage her to pray about it, as if that excuse for inactivity would get her out of a financial predicament. Even if God listened to prayers, he had better things to do than worry about a café that was going bankrupt.

The clock struck three, and still she was wide awake.

***

Nancy slept in on Friday morning, barely awake when Bruce left, and oblivious to the noise of the kids getting their own breakfast and slamming doors. She hurriedly showered and dropped the children off at Sarah's. Mary and Jaime were already there when she finally arrived at the café.

"Out late partying, eh boss?" Jaime asked. "I know how you feel. Me and Jennifer didn't get in until 2:00 ourselves. Well, we spent from midnight until two smooching on the porch, but I was sure awake for that. So is that your problem too?"

Nancy laughed. "Not exactly. It took me a while to get the kids ready this morning, that's all. Say, who's Jennifer? I thought you were going out with someone named Sylvia. Or was it Tiffany? I can't keep them straight."

"Yeah, neither can I."

Nancy wandered into the kitchen and watched Mary as she chopped some onion. "At least you were able to unlock the door today. Maybe we'll have a good day finally."

"Uh, I'm not too sure," Mary said.

Nancy's stomach knotted. "What now?"

"There was a message." Mary nodded toward the answering machine. "Some man from the county. Said they're coming out today for a health inspection."

"Oh, great." Nancy automatically surveyed the kitchen, looking for possible violations. She would need to hide the clutter on the desk and pretend she didn't do her paperwork here. The grill looked reasonably clean, and the cutting boards were washed and disinfected twice a day, but that didn't mean they couldn't find something wrong with them.

"Have you seen those signs?" Nancy asked. The regulations required hand washing signs in the restroom and in the kitchen, but Nancy had never gotten around to putting them up. Few people worked in her kitchen, and it seemed to her that a sign telling people to wash their hands was an insult to their intelligence.

"In the back room, probably," Mary said.

Nancy rummaged around and found them, still in the paper bag from the restaurant supply store. She got some tape and put them up. What else was there? The back room was full of cardboard boxes and supplies, and was undoubtedly a fire code violation. Did the health inspectors check for that, or did they leave it to the fire marshal?

"When were they coming?" she called out to Mary.

"Didn't say. Some time today."

A few customers showed up for lunch. One of them, a hiker, spread a wet raincoat and hat across the spare chairs at his tables. He loudly asked why there was no tofu on the menu, drank water, and ended up ordering only a bowl of chili. A young couple brought in their out-of-control children. The baby sat in a high chair and poured a cascade of crackers and soggy Cheerios onto the floor; the toddler wandered around the restaurant and screamed whenever his parents tried to make him stay in his seat, provoking glares from the hiker.

Finally at around two o'clock Mr. Clint Blackstone, county health inspector, arrived. He handed Nancy a business card, which seemed an unnecessary gesture when he had his photo ID—with the words HEALTH DEPARTMENT in huge red letters—clipped to his left shirt pocket. "Okay, let's have a look around," was all he said. She watched as he inspected the dining room, bending down to look at the table surfaces and making notes on his clipboard.

She followed him into the kitchen. He pulled a digital thermometer from his pocket and placed it in the refrigerator.

"Hey Nancy!" a voice called from the front room. Katharine Regan was shaking an umbrella on the floor and trying to smooth her blond hair. "Are you here?"

"Yeah. Right here," Nancy said. Katharine slid her glasses down and looked over the wet lenses.

"The place is empty! What did you do, poison some more people?" she asked loudly.

"Shhh!"

"What?"

"The *health inspector* is here!" Nancy whispered.

"Oh." Katharine grinned. Louder: "Hey, did you finally kill that rat in your kitchen? You know, the one that kept getting into the potatoes you kept under the sink?"

"Are you *crazy??* Be *quiet*." Nancy pushed her into a chair. "What are you talking about, rats and poison?"

"Yeah, that must be it. RATS and POISON. And all the ROTTEN FOOD that SPOILED."

Inspector Blackstone poked his head out the kitchen door and stared at Katharine, who began giggling uncontrollably. He shook his head and disappeared.

"You saw his car outside, right?"

Katharine pulled off her glasses and wiped the tears from her eyes. "Yep. It was a truck, actually. Why does a health inspector need a truck, do you suppose?"

"You turkey. That's the kind of thing that Isaac would do."

"Yeah, I've been hanging around him too much."

"Well, it's been a tough week. I don't have much

of a sense of humor left. Did he—"

"Tell me about the lock? Yeah, he did. Sorry about that. When I heard, I went right out and pulled my account from the bank. And talked a bunch of the other businesses into doing the same."

"You didn't! That's Bruce's bank!"

"I know. Just kidding."

Nancy slumped in her chair. "You're something else today."

"Just trying to cheer you up. Life goes on, you know. See, you're back in business."

"You call this business? I notice *you* haven't ordered anything."

"Mmm, good point. I'll have a roast beef, baked potato, Caesar salad, a half baguette of French bread and a glass of Beaujolais, please."

"How about a mug of stale coffee?" Nancy pushed herself up.

"Sure. That's what I wanted."

The sound of rattling plates came from the kitchen. The dishwasher turned on, then abruptly stopped. Nancy just shrugged when Katharine looked at her.

"Hey, I heard you came in and talked to Pastor Dave."

"Uh, yes, I did. I thought that was supposed to be private, sort of like the attorney-client privilege thing." Nancy slid the coffee in front of Katharine and sat down.

"Oh, don't worry. He just said you were in. I assumed you were talking about your thing with the prayer chain."

"Uh huh."

Katharine raised her eyebrows, but Nancy decided not to elaborate. Too complicated, and it was the least of her worries now. The kitchen door opened abruptly and the inspector came out, frowning.

"So? Did I pass?"

"No, ma'am. I'm afraid I'm going to have to shut you down."

"You're joking!"

"Not at all. The temperature in your cooler must be below forty degrees. I measured it at fifty, and you are storing eggs, ground beef, and other products that must be chilled below forty degrees Fahrenheit." He signed a form and pulled it off his clipboard. "I am required to close your establishment until you can verify that the equipment has been repaired and is functioning properly."

"Now, wait a minute. I check the temperature, too, and it's usually in the high thirties. Hey, you know what happened? I bet Mary had the door opened and closed a lot, putting away the lunch ingredients. And she probably put the soup stock in there. Did you see a big pot?"

"Who is Mary?"

"My cook. Come on, let's check the temperature again. I bet it's going down."

He hesitated. "All right."

Katharine followed them in. Inspector Blackstone put his thermometer in the refrigerator and then waited.

"So. You find anything else?" Nancy asked.

He shuffled through the notes on his clipboard and frowned again. "No, I'm afraid not."

"Well. That's a good thing, isn't it?"

"You have a fire and life safety issue with the rear exit. Too much material stored there. But that is out of my jurisdiction, I'm afraid."

Ha, I guessed right on that one, Nancy thought.

"When was the halon extinguishing system on

your grill last maintained?"

"I don't know. It's only a year old."

"It should be all right, then. Do you typically allow your customers in your kitchen?" He looked at Katharine.

"No, not typically. Say, did you wash your hands before you touched all my stuff?"

He grunted and opened the refrigerator and squinted at the thermometer.

"What's it say?"

"Forty-two. It has come down fairly quickly, actually."

"There, I told you."

"It is still a violation. It must be forty or below. Still, I am now unable to shut you down."

"Aw, shucks," Katharine said. Nancy poked an elbow in her ribs.

"You don't happen to work in the food preparation business here in town, do you ma'am?" he asked Katharine.

"No. Why?"

"Aw, shucks," he said, and made an almost imperceptible smile. He handed Nancy a form and left the kitchen without another word.

"See ya, Katharine," his voice called from the front room. The door rattled shut.

Nancy stared at her. "How does he know your name?"

Katharine grinned. "He's my brother-in-law."

"You're kidding. But his last name was Blackstone or something."

"Yep. He's my older sister's husband. Sort of a nerdy guy, but he does have a sense of humor. Well, a dry sense of humor, at least."

Nancy laughed. "Come on, let's sit down. Your coffee's getting cold." They went back to the main room. "Why didn't you tell me you knew him?"

"I don't know. Just kidding around."

"Well, at least he wouldn't have really shut me down."

"Oh, I don't know about that. He does get into his job." She sipped her coffee and watched the traffic out the window. "So," she said, changing the subject. "Dave said he invited you to church on Sunday. Gonna come?"

Nancy wasn't prepared for the question. "We'll see."

"We'd love to have you join us."

She made what she hoped sounded like a noncommittal murmur. Her parents had dragged her to church a few times when she was a child. She remembered the musty hymnals and singing unfamiliar songs to the accompaniment of a pipe organ and the warbling of an obese soprano in the choir. They would send her off to Sunday school in the middle of the service where she would sit with girls in dresses and boys with slicked-down hair and do craft projects involving paper cut-outs of ancient people in robes and sandals. She would count the minutes until the rumbling of the organ pump signaled the last hymn for the congregation upstairs, and a merciful rescue by her parents.

She had had an even worse experience as a teenager, when she had visited a cousin in California. He had talked her into attending a church that he had recently discovered, where they sang the same song over and over again, hands in the air, for what seemed like hours. To her horror, they made the guests stand up and introduce themselves, and stuck her with a name tag. When the service finally ended, an earnest friend of her cousin came up and bluntly asked her when she had been saved. She had felt like saying "I will be as soon as I can get back into my car," but instead gave a vague response and stared at her cousin, imploring him to get her out of there.

"The early service starts at 9:00," Katharine said helpfully. "That's when we go, especially in the summer."

"Uh huh. We'll see."

***

On Sunday morning Nancy heard birds singing and opened her eyes to a stray ray of sunshine painting the far wall and thought she was safe. But when she rolled over the clock read 7:15, far too early. She forced herself to keep still, and listened for Bruce's steady breathing. If he awoke, he would spring out of bed, ready to get the day started.

Later—it seemed like an hour had gone by—she heard the beeping of a video game and knew that Jake was up. She slowly tilted her head and looked at the clock. It was only 7:35.

She dozed off and when her eyes opened again it was 8:30 and Bruce's side of the bed was empty. She knew that by the time she was dressed and finished with breakfast, it would be 9:30, too late to make it to the church service. She got up and turned on the shower water, wondering where this fixation on going to church was coming from.

Bruce had cooked French toast and Jake and Indigo were already digging in when Nancy joined them.

"How about we take a drive, get out of this wet

weather?" Bruce asked.

"How far do we have to go, Arizona?" Nancy forked a piece of toast onto her plate and poured a dab of syrup on it.

"Is that where Disneyland is?" Jake asked.

"No, that's in California. The weather report said it should be sunny in central Oregon today. I thought we could go over to Otter Lake. Maybe rent a boat."

"Yeah! Can we go tubing?" Jake asked.

"No, the lake's too small. But we can go fishing."

"Oh," Jake said, without much enthusiasm.

"And you could swim off the boat."

"That's what I want to do," Indigo said. "But I don't want the fish to eat me."

"They will 'cause you look like a worm," Jake said.

He ran from her, laughing, as she chased him into the family room.

It was nearly ten before they got the children fed, dressed, and loaded into the van. Nancy was hit with a feeling of foreboding as they headed east from Cedar Creek. It must be the business, she thought. She had gone in for a while on Saturday, but there were few customers and not much for her to do. She thought of sending Michelle home to save money, but that wasn't fair to the girl, and there was a chance it would get busier some time.

As they rounded Mount Hood and dropped down the east side of the Cascades the clouds began to break up, and sunlight filled the van. The children, who had been relatively quiet, started to chatter and joke with each other. Bruce hummed a tune and tapped a beat on the steering wheel.

They rounded a corner and Nancy saw a blur move through the trees by the side of the road. Bruce suddenly slammed on the brakes and the van skidded, tires squealing. The seat belt dug into her shoulder, and she felt a thud as the car hit something. The van came to a stop sideways in the road and for a moment there was complete silence.

Then Maddie screamed. "He's dead!"

Nancy tried to turn around in her seat, but she was pinned by the seat belt. She fumbled for the latch and released it. Jake had been sitting in the middle seat with Maddie, and Nancy whipped around to check him out. She felt a searing pain in the base of her neck as she turned, and ignored it.

Jake was looking at her, wide eyed. Maddie's nose was pushed against the side window.

"He isn't moving. Can we save him?" she said.

"Are you all right back there?" Nancy asked. Indigo and Sam nodded.

"Yeah," Jake said. "What happened?"

"We must have hit an elk," Bruce said. He slowly got out of the car. The front of the hood was crumpled, and he managed to push it free of its latch. He stood under it for a minute and all Nancy could see was his hand. She tried to roll down her window but the switch wasn't working.

"Can I see if he's breathing?" Maddie asked.

"Hold on," Nancy said.

"The radiator's smashed into the fan," Bruce said. "We'll have to push the van to the side of the road."

Nancy got out. Bruce had her steer, and he pushed from behind. She saw the elk lying in the ditch, a smear of blood on its side.

"How are we going to get to the lake?" Jake asked.

Nancy didn't answer. She pulled her cell phone from her purse and turned it on. The signal was weak, but worth a try. She punched in Katharine's number and waited while it rang. The answering machine came on, and Nancy remembered that Katharine would still be in church. She tried the café, and reached Ernesto the weekend cook. He looked up the number of a tow operator in Government Camp for her and she wrote it on a scrap of paper she found in the glove compartment. The dispatcher said the next available tow truck would take at least 45 minutes to get there.

"Can we get out?" Maddie said.

"I have to pee," Sam said.

"All right, you can get out, but stay off the road. Sam, you can go in the trees."

Maddie inspected the elk. "I think he's breathing."

Bruce herded the kids across the ditch into the shade of the fir and pine trees, and sat on a rock. A pickup truck with a camper whooshed by without slowing. The hiss of its tires was slowly replaced by the clicking of grasshoppers and the twittering of small birds.

"Is anybody hungry?" Nancy asked.

"I am!" Sam said.

"I thought we were going to have a picnic on the boat," Jake said.

"Sorry buddy. It doesn't look like we're going to make it to the lake today," Bruce said.

"Can we take the deer to a vet?" Maddie asked.

"It's an elk," Bruce said, "and I don't think there's much life left in it."

Nancy carried a basket and small cooler from the

back of the van. Indigo wordlessly took a peanut butter and honey sandwich and a carton of juice. The others lined up behind her to paw through the picnic basket.

After he had finished his sandwich, Jake rummaged in the van and pulled out a slingshot he found under a seat. He set his empty juice container on a stump and began to shoot rocks at it.

"Let me try!" Sam pleaded.

"Okay, but you have to find your own rocks," Jake said. Nancy watched and fought back a tear. Normally at this time of year they would be taking a family vacation. Last year it was a car trip to Yellowstone and Glacier parks. They had talked about renting a place in the San Juan Islands, or maybe a week in the Sawtooths in Idaho, or even a trip to Disneyland. But she had ruined those plans with a business that was consuming their disposable income and her time, with no end in sight. She should just sell the thing, but at this point she seriously doubted anyone in their right mind would want to buy it. And she couldn't afford to just walk away from it; they had so much of their personal assets securing the bank financing that it would probably plunge them into bankruptcy. It was a mess, a stinking mess.

The kids were bored and complaining when the tow truck finally arrived. They were momentarily amused as the 300-pound truck driver hooked the chains to the van and winched it up onto the flatbed.

"Can we ride back there?" Bruce asked.

"Where's that you mean? Like, in your car?"

"Yeah."

He grunted and shook his head. "No way."

"So how are we supposed to get home?"

"Hey, my problem is your car. The rest is your

problem. I can take a couple of you up in the cab, but that's it. Maybe you can hitch hike or something."

"Great. We've only seen a dozen cars or trucks since we've been standing here, and who can take six passengers?"

The tow operator shrugged and wiped his hands on greasy overalls. "Where do you want me to leave this thing?"

Bruce gave him directions to Moe's Auto Shop in Cedar Creek. They watched in silence as the truck pulled away with their van.

"What now?" Nancy said.

"I guess we'll hitch hike like he said. We can split up if we have to—I'll take the girls and you take the boys."

They sat and waited. A truck pulling a boat sped by, ignoring Bruce's thumb. Maddie inspected the elk again and admitted it wasn't breathing anymore. Sam and Jake started digging roads into the hillside with sticks. Indigo tried making a daisy chain with tall grass.

Ten minutes later a Ford Explorer followed by a Honda Civic drove by, but from the wrong direction. They made a U-turn a hundred yards down the road and pulled over onto the shoulder.

"Need a ride?" Katharine Regan called from the Civic. Her husband waved from the Ford.

"What are you guys doing out here?" Nancy asked.

"We went to the Fir Away after church, and Ernesto said you might be stuck out here."

"Well, we're sure glad to see you. But how did you know if we had already hitched a ride?"

"Took a chance. Besides, it was an excuse to go

find some sunshine."

They loaded the picnic basket and cooler into the Explorer. Nancy and the girls joined Katharine in the Honda. Nancy leaned back in the seat and exhaled slowly.

"It is so good of you to come," she said quietly.

Katharine looked over at her. "Hey, it's no problem. You would have done the same for me."

"Yeah. Still."

As they approached the Barlow Summit on Highway 35 they entered clouds, misty at first, then wisps of white and finally a thick blanket of moisture that forced Katharine to leave her wipers on. As they plunged down the mountain west of Government Camp the clouds swallowed them in a dark tunnel of gloom, splattering the windshield with heavy drops. Nancy leaned against the window and closed her eyes, hoping for sleep.

11

"Why does your house smell funny, grandma?"

"What's that, dear?" Betty Scruggs asked, bending down to hear. Behind her, her son, Harold Junior, put a finger to his lip and shook his head. The child looked at him in confusion.

"I said, why does your house smell funny," the child practically yelled. He called her "grandma," but Betty was actually his great-grandmother. He was Harold Junior's grandson, temporarily being raised by Harold and his wife while their daughter went through rehab or whatever it was this month.

"Oh! That must be the cabbage I'm cooking for dinner. I guess that would smell funny to you. Doesn't Jean cook it for you, Junior?"

"Not much," Harold said, talking near her ear. It could be the cabbage, or it could be the septic system backing up again. He didn't understand how she could put up with it.

Jean came in from the car carrying a fruit salad, and the strawberry pie she had brought for dessert.

"Here, let me take that for you," Betty said.

"I've got it, Mom. I'll just put it on the kitchen counter." She squeezed past. "Did you finish that afghan you were working on?" Jean said over her shoulder.

Betty didn't answer. Jean repeated, louder. "Mom, did you finish the afghan? The one with the pretty blue and pink yarn?"

"Oh, yes. Here, let me show you." Betty shuffled into the living room. Harold began to follow, and then noticed that his grandchild had discovered an eggbeater in the kitchen. Standing on tiptoes, he reached into the sink with both hands and began furiously spinning the beater. A spray of soapy water shot through the air.

"Alec! Stop that!" Harold rushed in and took a face full of dishwater before he could disarm the child. "Now help me clean this up." He handed a dish towel to his grandson, who made a feeble attempt to dab up some of the water on the counter. Harold took another towel and leaned over to dry the window. By the time he was done, Alec had stuck his towel in the back of his shirt collar to make a cape, and was running back and forth from the kitchen to the dining room.

"I'm batman!" he yelled.

They eventually got the food on the table and sat down to eat. Harold had just finished saying a blessing when the phone rang. "I'll get it," he said.

"Hello? This is Shirley Finn from the Cedar Creek Church. I'm just calling with a prayer request for Betty."

"Okay. Just a minute." Cupping the mouthpiece, he called out, "It's for you Mom. A prayer request, she says."

Harold waited as his mother slowly made her way to the phone.

"What was it?" Jean asked when Betty had returned.

"It was a prayer request. They want us to pray for Nancy McReigh's daughter. She has laryngitis."

***

After the church service, Mac O'Connor liked to treat himself to a lunch at the Snag Inn. He sat on a padded bench in a booth and worked his way through a plate of prime rib, baked potato heaped with sour cream, chives, and bacon bits, with a side salad and a cup of coffee. His children and grandchildren often invited him over on Sundays, but he found excuses and preferred the time alone. He pondered the sermon that Dave Montgomery had given, on humility. He agreed with most of what the young pastor had said—at least as much as he had been able to hear of it—and thought about how he could live a more humble life.

The pastor hadn't said anything about lemon meringue pie in connection with humility, so he ordered a slice from Mabel when she came by to top up his coffee. He savored the tart filling and crispy crust, and watched an infant in a high chair in the booth across the aisle throw his food onto the wood floor.

After he had paid and left a generous tip for Mabel, Mac drove a few miles into the countryside and pulled up in front of a metal-sided moss-covered single wide trailer. The door slapped open and two children burst out. Yuliana, age nine, was wearing a navy blue dress and old sneakers. Umberto, two years younger, wore a white shirt and threadbare black pants. It looked like he had just washed his hair, and his mother had combed it back. They slid onto the bench seat of the truck with him. Their mother waved from the door.

"Where are we going today, Mr. Mac?" Yuliana asked.

"To a ball game. Buckle your seat belts."

He parked at the Gateway transit center and they took the MAX light rail into the stadium in downtown Portland. The kids sat quietly during the ride and watched a homeless woman who muttered to herself, and a girl with pale white skin, purple hair, a ring in her nose and a live snake around her neck.

Mac bought them hot dogs and Cokes and waited as the Portland Beavers came onto the field.

"Have you ever watched a baseball game?" he asked.

"Oh, lots." Umberto said. Mac leaned over to hear him.

"Here?"

"No. At school mostly. And on TV."

Mac O'Connor had owned 600 acres of ornamental plant nursery in the outskirts of Cedar Creek. It was now managed by a son and daughter, but he kept in touch with the business. Six months ago one of the employees—Yuliana and Umberto's father—had been killed in a car accident. Their mother stayed to work in the fields and try to raise the children, but Mac knew how hard it was.

"Well, here's something you don't see on TV," he said. "Watch the left fielder—he's in a different place out there for every batter."

"How come they don't show it on TV?"

"Because they zoom in on the pitcher and the hitter. You never know what the other players are doing."

They watched as the first batter got a single, the second struck out, and a third walked.

"You're right," Umberto said. "How come the guy moves around like that?"

"The second batter was left-handed, so he would

probably pull the ball to the right. Then the fielder moved in a little for the third batter. I guess he figured he wouldn't hit as hard."

"Is he making a signal now?" Yuliana asked.

"What's that?" Mac squinted. He laughed. "No, he just has an itch."

The crowd roared as the next batter hit a triple, knocking two runners home. Yuliana said something, but Mac couldn't hear it over the noise.

After the game, Mac held their hands to keep them from getting lost, and from getting ahead of him. After sitting so long he limped; he wasn't able to walk fast even on good days. Back on MAX, the kids chattered to themselves and Mac watched dark gray clouds swirl over the city. He drove them back to their trailer. Yuliana gave him a hug. Her mother watched from the door. "Gracias," she called out.

Mac let himself into his house and sank into his rocker, ready to take a nap. Out of the corner of his eye, he saw the flashing red light of his answering machine. He tried to ignore it, and then felt guilty about it. He pushed himself out of the chair and limped over to the machine and hit the play button. There was only one message, a prayer request.

"Mac, this is Betty Scruggs calling from the prayer chain. We've been asked to pray for Nancy McKay's daughter. She has laryngitis."

Mac memorized it, then erased the message. He fell back into his rocker and closed his eyes.

***

Stephanie Ong and her husband were finishing the dinner dishes when the phone rang. But she didn't hear it. Sabrina had six girls over and they were in the adjoining family room, chattering and squealing in laughter.

"It's for you, Mom." Sabrina's sixteen-year-old hearing had immediately homed in on the sound of the telephone, and she had dived for it. The girls had quieted down, but as soon as Sabrina handed off the phone, the decibel level shot back up.

"Who was it?" he husband asked as she put the phone away.

"Mac O'Connor with a prayer request."

"Who for?"

"I'm not sure. Do you know someone named Nancy McKay?"

"Uh, no."

"Well, anyway. Her daughter has meningitis."

***

Nancy would have preferred to be closed on Mondays, like most of the other restaurants in Cedar Creek, but she didn't want to miss out on the business, and she certainly didn't want to lose her customers to fast food.

She watered the indoor plants—a few ferns and some other green things that had looked good out at the Blossom Nursery. Mary arrived, whistling the tune to "I Still Miss You Baby…But My Aim is Getting Better."

"So how was your weekend?" she asked.

Nancy paused. She had figured she would spare Mary the details. "Fine," she said.

"Me and John, we went down to the Saturday

Market. Got a little wet, but had a good time. I found a straw hat and John got a few presents for relatives." Mary's voice trailed off as she disappeared into the kitchen.

Nancy followed her. "So, how are you and John doing these days?"

"Great. It's like nothing happened. Well, we're really getting along better than ever, so maybe its more like nothing bad happened." She began to fill a huge pot under the sink. "We don't talk about it much, though. It was too weird."

"Yeah, I can understand that."

Nancy went through the opening routine, and waited for Jaime to arrive.

"Hey, did you see it?" he asked as he burst through the door.

"See what?"

"My new babe-mobile. It's parked right out front!"

"We're supposed to save that space for customers."

"Yeah, yeah. Come on."

She followed him outside. The babe-mobile was an old, slightly dented Geo Metro. "Looks good, Jaime," she lied.

"Well, it's wheels, anyway. Runs like a dream. I couldn't get Heather in the back seat last night, though."

"Heather?"

"Yeah. See, she's too tall to fit back there." He sighed.

"I thought you weren't supposed to drive yet."

"How come?"

She nodded toward his walking cast.

"Aw, what the doctor doesn't know won't hurt him. It's an automatic anyway, so I can drive with one leg just fine. Here, I'll show you."

He got in the car and parked it on the side street around the corner. Nancy shook her head and walked back into the café. She mixed up a pair of mochas in take-out cups, added whipped cream and a dash of cinnamon, and pushed on the lids.

"I'll be back in fifteen minutes," she called out to Mary.

Katharine was at the counter talking on the phone when Nancy walked in to the Discovered Treasures Shop.

"I brought you a present," she whispered. "Where's Marge?"

Katharine motioned toward the back.

Marge was bent over, polishing a brass flower pot.

"Hey Marge, want a mocha?"

She straightened slowly. "Why, sure." She took the cup and pried the lid off and took a sip. "Katharine told me about your adventure yesterday. Good thing no one was hurt."

Nancy rubbed her neck. "Yeah. The elk was, though."

"That's the way it goes."

It sounded like Katharine had finished her phone conversation, and Nancy made her way through the crowded shelves to the counter. Katharine was already sipping on her mocha.

"So. Any word on your van?"

"They said they could fix it. Don't have an estimate yet, but it doesn't matter. We have a thousand dollar deductible. I need it back, though. I had to walk to work today."

"It's good for you."

"Yeah. So's an enema."

Katharine laughed.

"Well, I have to get back to the café," Nancy said.

"Hey. Thanks for the mocha."

When she returned, she was surprised to find a table full of customers. They looked like hikers, pouring over trail maps and drinking coffee.

"Sarah called," Mary said. "Wants you to call her."

The kids are probably trying to talk her into taking them to the zoo or something, Nancy thought. She went back to the kitchen and dialed.

"It's Indigo," Sarah said. "She says she isn't feeling well, and she does have a slight temperature. About a hundred."

Great, Nancy thought. "What's she doing now?"

"She's just lying down on the couch in the living room. She says she doesn't need anything. She doesn't even want to watch TV."

"Okay. She'll probably be all right, but thanks for calling. Let me know if she gets any worse."

After a while the hikers left, and then the first lunch customers started trickling in. Nancy helped Jaime take orders, but he could have handled it by himself.

She was sitting on a stool behind the counter, waiting for the credit card machine to spit out a receipt, when she heard a squeal from the kitchen. A soon as she was done with her customer, she rushed through the door.

"What's the matter?"

"Look!" Mary was mopping water from the floor. From somewhere under the dishwasher, steaming soapy water bubbled up.

"Let's shut off the dishwasher," Nancy said.

"I already did. The water kept coming."

Nancy lifted the bar that opened the front of the washer. Suds dripped off the rows of plates and a pool of water beneath them slowly receded.

"Looks like the drain pipe got plugged up. I'll have to rinse these in the sink." Nancy slid the tray over to the sink and squeezed the handle for the overhead spray nozzle.

"Uh oh," she said.

"What?"

"This sink's backing up too. Maybe the whole sewer line is stopped up."

"What are we going to do? We still have a couple of tubs of silverware to run through."

Nancy watched as the water level sank. "Maybe I can do a few of them by hand in here. I think we have enough clean stuff to get us through the rest of lunch, anyway."

"By hand! It will take forever!"

"You're too modern, Mary. I bet they always used to do them by hand, years ago."

"Huh. I would have just used plastic, then."

Nancy laughed. "I guess I better call a plumber."

The plumber, a local Roto-Rooter technician, promised he would be out "some time before six." The visit would be a minimum of sixty dollars, cash. Nancy had to make sure there was enough in the till.

She had put down the phone when Jaime stuck his head in the kitchen. "Uh, a customer said there's a problem with the restroom."

"Oh, no," Nancy said. "I forgot about that."

"Come again?"

"The sewer pipe seems to be plugged up. I forgot it would affect the bathroom too. Did it flood the floor?"

"Dunno. I was afraid to look."

Nancy took the mop and bucket into the restroom. The mess wasn't as bad as it could have been, but she would have to put an out-of-order sign on the door.

"Well, it could be worse," Mary said.

"Yeah? How?"

"The health inspector could've chosen today for his visit."

***

Indigo was lethargic when she stopped by at Sarah's house. "Have you eaten anything, hon?" Nancy asked.

"No." The reply was quiet.

"Well, I'll get you home and mix up some hot chocolate, okay?"

"All right."

Once Indigo was tucked into her bed, Nancy rummaged around for their digital thermometer. She hadn't needed to use it for a couple of years, but it still seemed to work. Indigo's temperature was a hundred and two. "I'll get you some aspirin, baby," Nancy said, stroking her forehead.

"All right."

Bruce was on time coming home, and helped prepare dinner. He cooked hot dogs on a gas grill on the back porch, tucked under the eves to stay dry. Nancy told him about the plumbing problem and the café. The plumber had cleared it just before she left for home. "Grease, probably," he said. "Happens all the time in restaurants." She had protested that they hardly used any grease, but he had just shrugged.

He went in and checked on his daughter as Nancy finished setting the table.

"She says she isn't hungry," he said, returning to the kitchen. "Poor thing."

"Yeah. Probably the flu or something. I'm not surprised, as crummy as this weather has been."

"The other kids are feeling okay, though?"

"Yes, so far at least."

"What's for dinner?" Maddie asked, sitting at the breakfast table and clutching an old Game Boy.

"Tube steaks," Nancy said.

Maddie muttered something, but all Nancy could hear was a series of mechanical beeps and whistles from the game.

After dinner they watched TV for a while, then Nancy and Bruce escaped to the quiet of the living room. Bruce read the morning's Oregonian, and Nancy skimmed a Sunset magazine, looking for new recipes. At nine thirty she herded the kids out of the family room and into their pajamas. While they were brushing their teeth, she checked on Indigo again.

She was asleep, breathing softly. Nancy felt her forehead. It seemed about the same as it had earlier. She tucked her in and kissed her on the top of the head.

Nancy and Bruce relaxed in the living room for a little longer, until she realized she had read the same paragraph in her magazine three times through half-closed eyes. "I'm going to bed," she said.

"I'll join you soon," he replied.

Later, something made her wake up. The house was quiet and Bruce was asleep beside her. The bedside clock said it was just past two in the morning. She closed her eyes and tried to go back to sleep, but couldn't.

She put on a robe and turned on the hallway light. Indigo and Maddie's room was dark. She opened the door wider. In the gloom, it looked like Indigo's eyes were open.

"How do you feel, hon?" Nancy whispered.

"Not so good."

"Do you have a sore throat?"

"No. Not inside."

"What do you mean?"

"I don't know."

"Do you have a headache?"

"Yeah. And my neck hurts. It feels…I don't know…tight or something."

"Hmm."

"I'll get you some more aspirin."

"Okay."

She began to go to the bathroom medicine cabinet, then paused and changed her mind. In a kitchen drawer she dug around for a phone number.

"Mt. Hood Hospital advice nurse. How can I help you?"

"I'm not sure. My daughter isn't feeling very well, and I just thought I should call."

"Okay. How old is she?"

"Five."

"And what are her symptoms?"

"She has a temperature, around a hundred and two the last time I checked. No appetite. Head ache. And she says her neck hurts."

There was a pause at the other end. "Does she have any sort of rash?"

"I don't know. I'll check." She carried the phone into the girls' bedroom and turned on the light. Maddie groaned and rolled over, covering her head with a pillow. Indigo watched her silently as she pulled down the sheet and lifted her pajama shirt. A faint cluster of red dotted her chest.

"Yes," she told the nurse. "It doesn't look like the measles, but it looks like some kind of rash."

"Ma'am, you need to bring her in."

"All right. When do you open in the morning?"

"No, I mean right now. Don't even take time to get dressed. You need to get her here immediately. Go directly to the emergency room. They'll be waiting."

"Don't you need to know my name?"

"There will be time for that later. Now, go."

12

"I'll go with you," Bruce said.

"No, you should stay with the others."

"I'll call a sitter."

"At this hour? I don't want to wait that long, anyway. The nurse sounded pretty worried."

"What do you think it is?"

"I don't know. Maybe some bad sort of flu is going around."

Nancy pulled on jeans and a sweatshirt and stuck her feet in sandals, then got Indigo up.

"Can you walk, hon?" Nancy asked.

"Okay." She took a few uncertain steps, and looked at her mother in a silent plea for help.

"Here, let me carry you." Nancy cradled her in her arms, and carried her into the garage, carefully placing her into the front seat of Bruce's car. There was hardly any traffic and downtown Cedar Creek was dark as she sped through it. The fifteen miles of rural highway between Cedar Creek and the hospital seemed endless.

She pulled up in the sallyport at the emergency room entrance and went around to open Indigo's door. As she carried her through the entrance, a tall man in blue hospital scrubs hurried up to meet her.

"They said to bring my daughter in--"

"I know," he said quickly. "Come with me."

The nurse led them to an examining room, and gently took Indigo from Nancy's arms, setting her on a paper-covered bed. He put a thermometer in her mouth, and took her blood pressure.

"What does she have?" Nancy asked.

"The doctor will be here in a minute. We'll see."

A woman in a white coat and a stethoscope around her neck came in and glanced at the chart that the nurse had begun filling in. She pulled up a chair and held Indigo's hand.

"How does your neck feel, sweetheart?" she asked.

"Stiff. I can't turn my head very well," Indigo said quietly.

The doctor nodded and lifted the pajama shirt. She made a note on the chart. "We'll need to get a lumbar puncture," she told the nurse. She gave some curt instructions involving medications that Nancy had never heard of.

"What does she have?" Nancy asked weakly.

The doctor stood and touched Nancy's elbow. "We'll have to run some tests to know. But her symptoms are consistent with meningitis. We can't afford to take any chances."

Nancy remembered reading about a teenager who had had meningitis a year ago. The child had died. Nancy's legs started to collapse and she leaned against the bed. "Oh. No."

"It can be treatable," the doctor said, calmly pulling a chair over for her. "You did well by bringing her in now, instead of waiting for morning."

It might have gone that way, Nancy realized

dimly. What had made her wake up in the middle of the night?

"What's a lumbar puncture?" she asked.

"A spinal tap. We diagnose meningitis by testing the spinal fluid."

"Is it going to hurt?" Indigo asked.

"You'll be fine," the doctor said. She rubbed Indigo's shoulder and then left.

A second nurse appeared, a young Asian woman. "Ma'am, could you come with me? We need to do some paperwork."

Indigo looked at her forlornly. Nancy hesitated. "Can't I stay with her a while?"

The male nurse said to Indigo, "What's your name, doll?"

"Indigo."

"Well, we'll take good care of you, Indigo. You can let your Mom go for a few minutes, can't you?"

She nodded.

"I'll be right back, hon," Nancy said. She kissed her daughter on the forehead and squeezed her hand.

The nurse led her through a series of hallways. The hospital was quiet, with just a background hum of the air system and the occasional beeping of monitoring instruments. The check-in counter was brightly lit. Nancy rummaged in her wallet for her insurance card and passed it over.

The paperwork probably didn't take long, but it seemed like an eternity. Nancy just wanted to get back to her daughter. She thought about using the pay phone to call Bruce, but there wasn't anything he could do, and she decided at least one of them needed to get some sleep.

"Is that your car parked outside, ma'am?" the

check-in clerk asked.

"Oh! Yeah." She had forgotten that she had left it sitting at the entrance.

"It's okay. We haven't had a lot of traffic out there tonight, thank God. But it would be good if you could park it."

Nancy noticed that she wore a small gold cross on a necklace. "Yes, sure," she said.

When she made her way back to the emergency room, Indigo had her eyes closed. An IV was taped to her small arm. Two nurses were preparing a gurney.

"What are you doing?"

"We're just going to move her to a regular room, where she can be more comfortable." He winked at Indigo. "You'll get your own TV."

They slid her onto the gurney and hung the IV bag onto a chrome pole. Nancy followed them through more hallways, then up an elevator. I'll never find my way out of here, she thought.

A sign above a corridor read "Pediatrics Ward." The lights had been dimmed. Nancy heard a child coughing.

Indigo had a room to herself. It looked familiar to Nancy, and she remembered that it hadn't been so long ago that she had been in another hospital room, with Mary Mowatt. The nurses got Indigo settled into her bed and re-hung the IV bag. One of them hooked the chart on the end of the bed. "If she needs to go to the bathroom, you can help her by carrying the IV for her. I know it's a nuisance, but that's the way it goes. Other than that, if you need anything, just push this button. And anyway, one of the nurses on the floor will be looking in on her from time to time."

Nancy nodded absently. As they left, she pulled a chair up to the bed.

"How are you doing, baby?" she said quietly.

"All right."

Nancy stroked Indigo's forehead and felt the heat from the little girl at her side. After a while, she leaned back in her chair and closed her eyes, realizing that she was too exhausted for her revulsion of hospitals to have kicked in. She slept, fitfully.

***

The glass behind the plastic blinds was still black when she opened her eyes. A young man in a white coat was doing something with the IV bag.

"What're you doing?" Nancy mumbled. She sat up and ran a hand through her tangled hair.

"We're upping the dose of her antibiotics," he said quietly.

"Did you get the results?"

He sat down on the chair. Indigo was still asleep. "Yes," he said. "It is meningitis, I'm afraid. The good news is that it's a form of bacteria, so it can be fought with antibiotics. It's not like a virus, where you just have to let the body do its thing. So we have her on a pretty heavy dose of medication, to try to knock it out of her system before it goes any farther."

"So what's the bad news?" There always is, with doctors, Nancy thought.

"Well, the bad news is that this can be a pretty nasty bug. With luck, she'll have a full recovery. She'll feel pretty lousy while we're fighting it, but she could come through fine. In a few cases, though, there can be some permanent damage."

"Like what?"

He hesitated. "I'm not saying this is going to happen. But you need to know what we might be up against. Some times there is some paralysis. In rare cases, there can be brain damage. And of course, in a few cases—the tiny fraction that makes the press—it can be fatal."

Nancy stared at the ceiling. "Why did it have to happen to her?"

"It's a communicable disease, but I know what you mean. It doesn't seem fair. Look, I mention the worst case scenarios only because I have to be honest with you. You did well, catching it relatively early, and I really have to say that her prognosis is good."

"Catching it early? She started feeling bad early in the day—yesterday, I mean. How much later could I have been?"

"I know," he said gently. "Don't blame yourself. She was still conscious when you brought her in. When they're already unconscious, then I get really worried."

Already unconscious?

***

Nancy listened to the sounds of the hospital and Indigo's soft breathing and tried to pretend she was somewhere else. When daylight began to filter through the window blinds she got up, taking care not to disturb the sleeping girl. She found her way down to the lobby and called Bruce.

She tried to be calm when she described Indigo's

plight, but her voice caught, and she barely suppressed a sob.

"I'm coming right down," he said.

There was nothing he could do, but she knew he had to be with his daughter, too. "Okay. What about the kids?"

"I'll have Maddie feed them breakfast and walk them over to Sarah's."

"All right. See you soon, hon."

"Yeah."

"Oh, and could you bring me some clothes?"

"Like what?"

"Well, a T-shirt. And a bra. All I have is this sweatshirt."

"Okay. Where do you keep that stuff?"

"Just dig around in the dresser. And I need some shoes."

"Shoes. You only have about twenty pairs. Which ones?"

"My white sneakers. And some socks."

There was silence on the line. Either Bruce was mentally making a list, or he was trying to think of a way to end the phone conversation before the list grew.

"No problem. Hang in there, baby."

She found a cup of coffee and a donut and carried them back up to Indigo's room. Her daughter's eyes were open.

"How do you feel, sweetie?"

Indigo didn't respond.

Nancy set her breakfast down, and caressed Indigo's forehead.

"How are you feeling?" she repeated.

"Bad," Indigo whispered. "I want to go home,

Mom."

"I know. I do too. But they're giving you medicine to make you feel better. And I'll stay with you, sweetheart. Daddy's coming too, in a little while."

Indigo closed her eyes.

"Do you want me to get you some juice or something?"

"No."

"Do you need to go to the bathroom?"

Indigo didn't respond. A moment later she said, "No."

Nancy pulled the sheet up and kissed Indigo's forehead, and wearily sat down to drink her coffee. She needed something to pass the time, and to take her mind off the battle that was taking placing in her daughter's body. She should have asked Bruce to bring a book.

A nurse came in and checked Indigo's vital signs, making notes on the chart.

"I asked her if she wanted any breakfast," Nancy told the nurse.

"What did she say?"

"She said no. She usually eats a huge breakfast—three bowls of cereal and two pieces of toast. I don't know where she puts it."

The nurse laughed. "Well, I can understand if she's off her feed right now. She's getting some nutrition off the IV, but it sure isn't as much fun as a bowl of Fruity Pebbles."

"Is she getting any better?"

"She's still running a fever. The doctor will be here in about an hour, and he'll check on her."

Nancy sat for a while after the nurse left. The noise level on the floor had increased—carts being wheeled with breakfast, voices, a child crying. She checked on Indigo, then went back downstairs in search of a gift shop. She bought a paperback novel, toothbrush and toothpaste, and went back up to Indigo's room to use the tiny bathroom. She looked like a wreck, with bags under her eyes, and she made a half-hearted attempt to brush the tangles out of her hair.

It suddenly occurred to her that Bruce would have no way of getting to the hospital—she had his car. She could go back out to Cedar Creek to pick him up, although she really didn't want to leave her daughter that long. She noticed, for the first time, that there was a phone in the room.

Maddie answered when she called.

"Is Dad there?"

"No, he left already."

"How? He doesn't have a car."

"Somebody drove up. I guess he got a ride."

"Oh. Well, how are you kids doing?"

"Fine. Jake spilled his juice."

"Did you clean it up?"

"Duh. We didn't leave it on the floor."

"Well, thanks. Thanks for looking after your brothers."

"Sure. When are you guys coming home?"

"I don't know, hon. As soon as we can. But your sister is a sick little girl. They're giving her lots of medicine to cure her."

"Oh."

"Well, be good at Sarah's house. If you need me, you can call." She read off the extension number that was taped to the phone.

"Okay. Bye Mom."

Bruce arrived a half hour later. Nancy hadn't realized how glad she would be to see him. He hugged her tight and told her that everything would be all right. Then he sat on the edge of the bed and watched Indigo. His eyes followed the IV tube up to the clear bag, and Nancy knew it bothered him as much as it did her.

"Poor thing. Has she been awake this morning?"

"Yes, for a little while," Nancy said. "She was pretty out of it, though."

Nancy went out to the nurse's station to get another chair. It was a tight squeeze in the small room. They talked until they ran out of things to say, and Nancy tried to read her novel. At some point, a woman came in and asked a lot of questions about who Indigo had been in contact with in the past week. Later, a doctor appeared and studied the chart, then examined Indigo.

"How is she doing?" Bruce asked.

"It's too soon to tell," the doctor said. "But I'm a little concerned that she isn't responding to the medication yet. She's been under a fairly strong dose for eight hours."

"Is there anything we can do?"

"Just what you're doing—being here for her. And pray."

"It's that bad?"

The doctor raised his eyebrows. "We can do a lot with medicine these days. But we can always use help."

***

By late afternoon Indigo had slipped into a coma. Nancy was beside herself. She paced the hallway outside the Intensive Care Unit feeling helpless and terrified.

Bruce tried to calm her, but she could tell he was distraught too. A stream of doctors and nurses passed through Indigo's room, but even they seemed powerless to do any good.

At eight o'clock Nancy told Bruce, "I can't take this any more." She rushed down to the car, wiping tears from her eyes.

13

She drove with one hand and used the other to punch numbers into Bruce's cell phone.

"Katharine, this is Nancy. I need to know where Bernice Burns lives."

"Is something wrong?"

Her voice had given her away. "I'll explain later. Do you have her address?"

"Yeah, I think so. We have a church directory. Hold on."

Nancy waited. She dropped the steering wheel to hit the turn signal, and almost ran into the curb as she turned onto an arterial.

"Here it is. I guess she's moved into the Green Acres retirement home."

A retirement home? Nancy had assumed she lived alone in a house. "All right, thanks."

"Do you know where it is?"

"Yes."

"Well, let me know if you need anything."

"Thanks Kat."

She put the phone down and stepped on the accelerator pedal.

***

The girl at the front desk said that Mrs. Burns was in room 122. Nancy knocked on the door and waited. She could hear a TV set, loud, and knocked again. After a minute, the door opened.

"Yes?"

"Mrs. Burns? I'm Nancy Mackay. I called you a while back. About the prayer chain."

"Oh! Yes! Won't you come in?"

Bernice Burns reminded Nancy of her grandmother, before she had died. Thinning gray hair curled in a monthly perm job, bifocal glasses in a gold wire frame, a plain flowered dress and flat-soled shoes. She walked with a stoop and cleared some magazines off a chair. "Here, sit down."

Nancy waited until the old lady sat down next to her. "I need to know something," she said abruptly. "Did you pray for my daughter?"

Mrs. Burns thought for a moment. "Why, yes! You're Nancy Mackay! I did not make the connection. And how is she now?"

"Not too good. What, exactly did you pray for?"

"For healing, of course. She has some kind of sickness, laryngitis, meningitis, something like that?"

"Yeah." There's a big difference, Nancy thought. If they were going to do it, why didn't they use laryngitis? "Do you remember when you got the prayer request?"

"Well, let me think. I was watching Murder, She Wrote, I believe. So that must have been Sunday. Two nights ago, I suppose."

"It figures," Nancy said quietly.

"Pardon me?"

"Well, she got it. Yesterday. After you prayed about it."

"What's that?"

"Meningitis."

"Oh! Is that serious?"

"I'm afraid she's going to die." Nancy tried to choke back a sob. She couldn't do it, and her shoulders shook as she cried.

Mrs. Burns reached across a frail hand and gripped her elbow. "There, there. Let me get you a tissue." She disappeared and came back with a box of Kleenex. "Here you are, dear."

Nancy rubbed her eyes and blew her nose. "How could you have done this?" she sobbed.

"I'm sorry. I truly am. We were only trying to help, you know."

"Yeah. A big help."

Mrs. Burns blinked behind her glasses, but didn't say anything. Finally: "Tell me about her. Tell me about your daughter."

"Like what?"

"What is her name? How old is she?"

"Indigo. She's only five. She's a tiny thing, but smart. I love all my kids, but she's my baby. I can't bear to lose her." Nancy felt another tear run down her cheek, and rubbed at it with her wadded up Kleenex.

"Where is she now?"

"Where? She's at the hospital. Mt. Hood."

"I see. Well, we'll just have to pray for her, now won't we?"

Nancy looked up. "I don't know how. And when you did it, it didn't seem to do much good."

Mrs. Burns nodded and said quietly, "It is all we *can* do, though. And you must never underestimate the power of it. Here, give me your hand."

Nancy could feel her bones under cold skin, but the touch was reassuring. The old woman bent her head down and closed her eyes. She took several deep breaths and sighed, and began to speak.

"Father, we ask for your healing touch for little Indigo. We ask for your power to fight the disease that is in her body. Make her well and restore her strength. Give her, Father, a full recovery, we ask this of you." She was silent for a moment. "And share your power with her doctors, to give them wisdom and guidance. And be with her family, with her mother and her father, and give them hope and support. These things we pray, Father."

There was a long silence. "It's your turn now, dear," Mrs. Burns said quietly.

"I don't know what to say."

"Just talk to him. He's right here with us, you know."

Nancy closed her eyes to hold back the tears. She bit her lip. Mrs. Burns squeezed her hand.

"Oh God," Nancy said, and choked up again.

"That's a good start," Mrs. Burns said gently.

"Please help me. Help my little girl. Help my Indigo. I need her. I need her back. Just help her." Nancy's throat tightened and she could say no more. She repeated the words in her mind, over and over, until she lost track of time.

"Amen," Mrs. Burns finally said, quietly, and gave Nancy's hand a final squeeze. They sat in silence for a moment. "Can I get you some tea?"

"I should be getting back to the hospital." Nancy wiped her eyes with a new tissue. "But that would be nice. I don't think I would be able to drive right now." She felt drained, but oddly peaceful. She watched as the old lady put a kettle on the stove and got out two china cups.

They sipped their tea in silence. Finally, Nancy stood. "Thank you," she said.

"I'm glad you came, dear. Would you allow me to continue to pray for your Indigo?"

"Sure. That would be nice."

"But you need to, too."

"Yes. I will." She meant it, this time.

She slipped out into the hallway. Her eyes followed the pattern of the carpet as she walked, but her mind was somewhere else.

"Nancy! Is that you, boss?"

She looked up and was startled to see a familiar face.

"Jaime? What are you doing here?"

"Uh, my grandma lives here. I was just visiting her."

She looked down at an empty white vase in his hand.

"She wanted me to bring her some fresh flowers," he said. "I grow them in the window boxes at our apartment."

"Oh."

"How about you? I've never seen you out here before."

"I was just visiting someone too. A lady. Bernice Burns."

"Ah, yeah, I know her. Nice old gal. Say, didn't you stay home with your daughter today? How is she doing?"

"Not too good."

"Oh. Well, I hope she's feeling better by

tomorrow. I was really scrambling today, with all the customers. The place was packed."

"Was it? Really?"

"Uh, no. Not exactly. But we still missed you."

Nancy was glad the hallway was dim. She was sure her eyes were red. "Well, I have to get going."

"See you."

"Yeah."

***

Bruce was slumped in a chair in the waiting room outside the ICU.

"Any change?" Nancy asked.

"No." Bruce said, and rubbed his eyes. "No change."

She collapsed into a chair. How could she have expected anything else? "Where is she?"

He nodded toward the hallway. "But they're only letting us see her for a few minutes every hour."

Nancy was silent for a moment.

"How are you holding up?" she asked.

He shrugged. "Where did you go?"

"I just drove around for a while."

This section of the hospital was grimmer than the pediatrics ward. Nancy looked around for some way to escape the nightmare. She pulled her book out of a bag by Bruce's feet and tried to read. The words didn't make any sense, and she closed her eyes.

Forty minutes later, a nurse appeared.

"Mr. and Mrs. Mackay? You can see her now"

"Any improvement?" Nancy asked.

"I'm afraid not."

Nancy wasn't prepared for the scene that greeted her. Instead of just the IV tube attached to her, Indigo's tiny body was connected to a collection of monitoring wires. An oxygen tube ran to her nose and her face was pale. Machines hummed, and one of them beeped slowly. It took a while for Nancy to realize it was monitoring her daughter's heart.

"Oh, my baby," she whispered. Bruce put an arm around her shoulder and pulled her to him.

"We're doing everything we can," a voice said gently.

Nancy turned. A doctor walked briskly to the monitors and made some notes.

"Are you sure?" Nancy blurted. "She's only gotten worse since I brought her in."

"Now sugar…" Bruce said, giving her another squeeze. Nancy shook out of his arm.

"Exactly what *are* you doing," Nancy said, trying to keep the hysteria out of her voice.

"We're administering high doses of ampicillin and ceftriaxone. Those are most effective at fighting meningitis. It's about all we can do."

"What are her chances?" Bruce asked.

The doctor hesitated. "We'll have to wait and see. But

I have to be honest: the chances are pretty slim."

"Chances of what? Survival? Or a complete recovery?" Bruce asked.

The doctor just held his hands out and shook his head.

Nancy felt the room spinning and leaned against the bed. She put a hand on Indigo's forehead. Once again, the words came to her in a silent prayer. Please God, bring my baby back to me.

The nurse escorted them back to the waiting room. They sat together in silence. Images of Indigo played through her head—as a one-year-old in Sweet Pea pajamas, as a toddler taking her first steps, and later, the frightened look in her eyes as Nancy dropped her off for her first day of pre-school. She tried to fight back the tears, but Bruce felt her crying and hugged her, wordlessly.

Finally, she lay down with her head on Bruce's lap and fell into a shallow sleep.

14

"Come on sugar, wake up." The words dimly registered in her consciousness. She opened her eyes and sat up abruptly.

"Why? What is it?"

"I don't know. She just said the doctor wants to see us."

"Oh no," Nancy moaned.

She tried to stand, but her legs gave out. Bruce put his hand under her arm and lifted most of her weight. They slowly followed the nurse into the ICU.

The doctor was at the bed, his back to them. Nancy was afraid to look. He turned when they approached, then moved out of the way.

"Hi Mommy," Indigo said softly. Her head was propped on a pillow, and there was a hint of pink in her cheeks. "Hi Daddy."

"Indigo!" Nancy bent and put both hands on her daughter's shoulders. "Oh baby, my baby."

"What time is it?" the little girl asked.

"Just after four," Bruce said.

"Four? It seems like I've slept longer than that."

"No, four in the morning."

"Oh."

The doctor stood to the side. Nancy looked at him,

questioning.

"She's still weak, as you would expect. She's gone through quite an ordeal."

"But….?"

"But otherwise, she seems fine. We'll have to do some more tests when she's had a chance to rest, but from what I can tell, her brain functions and nervous system seem to be unaffected."

"So the medication finally worked," Bruce said.

"The medication? I don't know. In my experience, she was much too far gone for that to have brought about this kind of recovery. Frankly, I wouldn't believe it if I wasn't seeing it with my own eyes. I have never heard of anything like this."

Nancy stood up and looked at him. "It was a miracle, then, wasn't it?"

"It must be," he said simply.

***

An hour later, they moved Indigo back to her room on the pediatric floor. She said she was hungry, but the nurse explained she couldn't have any solid food until they had run her through the MRI. She dozed on and off, but each time she awoke, her voice was stronger.

"Mom?" she asked around six thirty."

"Yes, sweetheart?"

"I *really* have to pee!" she whispered.

Nancy laughed.

"What's so funny?"

She wiped a tear from her eye. "I guess I'm just laughing for joy." She helped Indigo out of bed and carried her IV bag into the tiny bathroom. A mundane task had never held so much pleasure.

Bruce brought up donuts and coffee, and they waited while Indigo was whisked away for her tests. Nancy felt giddy with elation and exhaustion.

"We're really lucky, aren't we sugar?" Bruce said.

"No. It's more than luck." She hesitated, then said, "Do you know where I really drove to last night?"

He raised his eyebrows.

"I went to see Benice Burns. She's part of the prayer chain—"

"Ah, the prayer chain."

"No, hear me out. They had been praying for Indigo's meningitis *before* she even got it."

"Huh? That can't be true."

"Yes! It is!"

"But why would they do that?"

"Oh, I don't know. The original prayer request probably got garbled again—they were probably supposed to pray for someone else's daughter, maybe for a completely different reason. But whatever happened, Mrs. Burns told me that she had prayed for my daughter and her meningitis on *Sunday night*."

He put his forehead into his hand and rubbed his eyes with his palms. "That's just plain spooky."

"But that's not all," Nancy said gingerly.

"Oh?"

"Yeah. When I told her about it, she said she was sorry, that she hadn't meant any harm. And then we prayed for Indigo."

"We?"

"Yes. Just Mrs. Burns and me."

"Uh huh."

"And then the miracle happened."

Bruce sat up and looked at her eyes. He slowly nodded.

***

"Nancy?"

It was a familiar voice.

"Pastor Dave!" She introduced him to Bruce. "How did you know we were here?"

"Oh, one of my flock told me you might be." He looked at the empty bed. "I assume that's a good sign?"

"Yes," Bruce said. "They're just wrapping up some tests, but so far it seems she's okay."

"That *is* good news. How are you two doing?"

"Tired, but fine." And I can't wait to get out of these clothes and into a hot shower, Nancy thought, immediately regretting her selfishness.

A nurse rolled Indigo back in, in a wheelchair. The IV

tube was gone.

"She passed all her tests," the nurse said. "You can get her dressed and go home any time you want."

As if I would stay another second, Nancy thought. "How do you feel sweetie?"

"Fine, Mom. Let's go."

"I'll get out of your way," Dave Montgomery said. "But listen, it sure would be good to see you all with us next Sunday."

To her surprise, Bruce answered without hesitation. "We'll be there." He glanced at the rain driving against the window pane. "And do me a favor. Have your congregation do something about this weather."

"We'll work on it," Dave said, smiling.

***

Indigo said she was hungry for a taco, and Nancy offered to stop at a fast food place. No, Indigo had said, can't we get Mary to make me one at your restaurant? Nancy knew she looked like a wreck, but went along with it.

There weren't any customers there, anyway. Mary was glad to put together a custom order for Indigo, and Jaime sat with her while she ate.

"You were sick, huh?" he asked.

"Uh huh," she nodded, her mouth full of taco.

"What did she have?" Mary asked, when Nancy ducked into the kitchen.

"Bacterial meningitis," Nancy said.

Mary's hands froze over the sink. She stared at Nancy. "You're kidding."

"No, that's what it was. She was a sick little girl."

"Yeah. I hear that can be pretty bad."

"Mary, she was this close to dying."

"Oh, no. What happened?"

"I don't know, but she's okay now. All I can figure is, God saved her."

***

They arrived at the church at 9:25—early enough not to make a scene, but late enough not to have to stand around with strangers. Nancy saw several familiar faces, and most people welcomed them warmly, but without making a fuss over them.

When they entered the sanctuary, Nancy saw Katharine Regan standing in the aisle, scanning the congregation. When she saw them, she smiled and came over.

"I was hoping you would come," she said. "I saved you some seats."

To Nancy's relief, they weren't too close to the front. Katharine's husband shook Bruce's hand, and made some small talk about the latest dip in the stock market.

The service began and Nancy held her breath, hoping that they wouldn't have to stand up and be stared at. But no such fate awaited her, and she was surprised to see a drummer and guitar players join the pianist when the songs started. She realized she had expected to hear the hum of the organ bellows, but there was no organ at all.

They stood and sang, following the words projected on a big screen. She didn't recognize the songs, but some had catchy rhythms. Bruce was on her right, and Indigo was on her left, singing loudly. Nancy put her arm around her Indigo's shoulder and smiled at her.

One of the congregation members read from the Bible, or what Nancy assumed was a Bible. But it seemed to be in plain English, with no "thees" and "thous." It was a passage from one of the gospels—Luke—and quoted Jesus telling the story of how birds don't need to worry, but are beautifully dressed anyway.

Then Pastor Montgomery invited the children to come up front. All four of her kids stayed glued to their seats, but then Melissa Williams, one of Maddie's friends from school leaned into their pew and whispered, "Come on." They immediately sprang up and spilled into the aisle.

At the front of the sanctuary, the pastor got down on a knee, and asked the children questions. "What do you worry about, sometimes?" he said.

Nancy craned her neck to see.

"Monsters under the bed," one child said.

"Global warming," Indigo said, and the congregation laughed. Indigo grinned.

The pastor explained, simply, how worries and fears were okay, but that God wants children—and adults—to put their trust in him. He quoted a prayer that one of the older congregation members said at night: "Lord, take care of my problems and my worries while I'm asleep…since you'll be up all night anyway." Next to her, Nancy felt Bruce chuckle.

The kids disappeared willingly to Sunday School classes. The pastor led a prayer, thanking God for good things that had happened in the past week, and asking for help in the health and other challenges the congregation members were facing. Nancy closed her eyes even harder when he gave a simple word of thanks for Indigo's recovery. Bruce squeezed her arm.

During the sermon, Nancy felt her mind wandering a few times, and noticed that one of the older men a few rows up seemed to be nodding off. But then Dave started describing the kinds of burdens that people carry—in work, in running a business, in raising a family—and she began to pay attention. He didn't minimize or dismiss the burdens, and instead made the point, using a few more quotes from the plain-language Bible, that Jesus knew all along that the burdens were too much for people to carry on their own. Trust in me; I'm here for you, was his simple message.

Nancy sat back and looked at the cross at the front

of the sanctuary. Her shoulders felt light, as if a physical weight was being lifted from her. She looked over at Bruce. He winked at her.

15

"Sugar, you've got to see this."

"What's that?" she asked, rubbing the sleep out of her eyes.

"Look."

She propped herself on one arm and looked out the window. Over the tops of the trees, the sun was beginning to peek around the north side of Mount Hood."

"Mmm. Nice." The clock read 6:10. She fell back on her pillow.

"Didn't you notice something missing?" Bruce asked.

"Like what?"

"Clouds! There isn't a cloud in the sky." Bruce looked at her expectantly.

"How 'bout that," she said, and fell back asleep.

She got up at seven and had breakfast with Bruce. Jake joined them, energized by the light streaming in the window. "Sarah said if we had a sunny day, we could have a paintball war!" he announced.

"Really?" Nancy was concerned. The boys would be merciless with the girls if they ever got hold of guns that really shot things.

"Well, no, not really. I just wanted to see what you would say."

"Why don't you play Kick the Can instead?"

"What's that?"

Bruce laughed, and got up to finish getting ready for work.

When she walked to the café, the neighborhood streets were steaming in the sun. Beads of water sparkled on the lawns and on the leaves of trees, and birds bathed in puddles.

She heard a noise in the kitchen when she let herself in.

"What are you singing?" she called out to Mary.

"If the Phone Doesn't Ring, You'll Know It's Me," she said.

Nancy laughed. "What do you think of the weather?"

"Hey, it's about time. Probably won't last, though."

"No, I think it will," Nancy said.

Jaime hobbled in on his walking cast. "Hola, boss," he said. "Hey, if this weather keeps up, I'm gonna have to take Rachel to the beach. You'll have to let me have a day off, okay?"

"Sure," she said, and laughed. She watched him put out the place settings. "Jaime, sit down. I have something I want to ask you."

He looked at her suspiciously. "Sure boss." He pulled out a chair and fell into it.

Nancy sat across from him and leaned forward. "Now, I know it's none of my business. But there really isn't a Rachel, or whatever her name is today, is there?"

"No Rachel? What do you mean?"

"Here's what I mean. All this time you've been telling us that you've been having these hot dates, but really, the woman you've been spending time with in the evening is eighty years old, right?"

He dropped his eyes to the table. "No, that's not right," he said.

"Are you sure?"

"Yeah. She's eighty-four."

Nancy laughed. "So why the charade?"

"I don't know. What would people think if they knew I was hanging out with my granny?"

She put her hand on his shoulder. "I don't know about other people, Jaime, but I think it's wonderful."

"Huh."

"No, really I do. It must mean so much to her."

"Yeah, I guess. But you have to promise."

"What's that?"

"Not to tell."

***

The traffic hit at ten-thirty. Later, Nancy figured out that that was about how much time it would take to throw fishing poles in the trunk, or hitch the camper up, and get on the road from Portland. But whatever the explanation, a steady stream of boats, campers, and recreational vehicles rolled by her café. And enough of them stopped that by eleven thirty every table was taken.

A cacophony of conversation and clinking silverware filled the main room. Jaime hustled from table to table, and Nancy kept up a steady stream of drinks and salads. The place actually started to heat up, and Nancy turned on the window air conditioner for the first time that summer. She held her breath, and to her amazement it hummed into life without protest.

Mary was harried but happy in the kitchen. The griddle sizzled with hamburger patties, breaded fish, and grilled sandwiches. The cash register rang, and continued its music into the early afternoon.

"Wow," Jaime grinned when they finally got a break.

"Why are you so happy? You must be exhausted, what with your bad leg," Mary said.

"Yeah, but it's great for tips. Look at this!" Nancy had added up the cash and credit card tips on a piece of paper that he was now waving at Mary.

"Seventy-five bucks!" she said. "That'll buy some gas for your junker."

"Excuse me, that fine vehicle is my babe-mobile," he said, and gave Nancy a knowing look.

The phone rang and Nancy paused before answering it, wondering if it was an unpaid vendor or some other creditor. But it was Bruce.

"Hey, the shop called and said your van is ready," he said. "If you want, I can get off work early, and we can go pick it up."

Nancy had wanted to stay for the dinner shift, to see if the customer traffic continued, but she knew she needed to be home with her family. "Sure," she said. "I'll just meet you over there."

"How are you going to get there?"

"I'll just walk. It's a gorgeous day."

***

After dinner they all walked over to the park and started a game of soccer. Other neighborhood kids began to join them and soon they had twenty children of all ages and two dogs on the field, with a mixture of laughter, yelling, and barking. Indigo was playing defender, and one of the older boys kicked a hard shot toward the goal. Nancy held her breath, thinking that Indigo was going to try to stop it with her head. But at the last second she ducked, and let the ball fall into the goalkeeper's arms. She caught her mother's concerned look, and just laughed and shrugged. Sam and Jake, covered with mud and grass stains from sliding tackles, helped take the ball up field. Nancy and a red-haired six-year-old boy tried to stop their progress, and Sam weaved through with ease, passing the ball off to Maddie. She deftly crossed it to another girl, who popped it into the goal. Maddie leaped into the air, whooping.

Nancy bent over, trying to catch her breath. When she straightened, she noticed it was nine o'clock and it was still bright out. The sun peaked from behind a single small gold-rimmed cloud, sending broad rays across the sky to the eastern horizon.

"Look at that," she said to Bruce, between gasps of breath.

He looked up at the sun. "Yeah. How about that, huh?"

16

Nancy sat in Dave Montgomery's office, trying not to stare at the plastic Bart Simpson figure.

"Go ahead, be my guest," the pastor said.

"How did you know?" she asked, and pulled the arm.

"I didn't do it! Lisa made me do it," the little Bart said.

Dave chuckled. "The spirit is willing, but the flesh is weak, right?"

"Yup," Nancy said, popping a red M&M into her mouth. "'Specially where chocolate is concerned."

"The woman made me do it, said the serpent," Dave said, and pulled the arm.

"Nice try, Homer," little Bart said.

Dave chewed on his M&M for a moment.

"So, how did you like the service?" he finally asked.

"I, uh, liked it," Nancy said. She wasn't sure of the protocol for describing a church service. Did you use the same adjectives as for a movie? Moving? Entertaining? Well-cast?

"Think you'll come back next Sunday?"

"Oh, yes. Definitely."

"Well, that's great. Great." He smiled. "But that's

not the reason I asked you to stop by. Well, not the <u>only</u> reason, anyway."

"Oh?"

"Yeah. C'mere, check this out." He stood up and led her into the secretary's adjoining office. On a credenza was an over-sized telephone set.

"An answering machine?" Nancy wasn't sure what the significance of it was.

"No, a phoning machine. I can program it through my computer, and we can put in a voice message that goes to as many people as we want." He looked at her as if she was supposed to figure out a mystery.

"Oh, I know! The prayer chain."

"That's right. We can put in the original prayer request, and it goes directly to everybody in the prayer chain. So I guess we can't really call it a chain anymore. I got the gizmo from one of the congregation members who works for a telemarketing outfit. Maybe we need to call it a Teleprayer Ring or something like that, huh?"

Nancy laughed. "What if it gets a busy signal?"

"It just waits a while and calls them back. It's very patient."

"But doesn't that take some of the fun out of it for the people who like to…well…"

"Gossip?" He led her back to the table in his office. "By the way, do you want some coffee?"

"No thanks—had too much already this morning back at the shop."

"Anyway, the answer is yes. It does take away some of the personal touch, and the benefit of people connecting with each other. I got a bit of a backlash at the meeting."

"Meeting?"

"Yeah. We convened all the members of the prayer chain on Sunday afternoon, after the worship service."

"Really?" Nancy felt a little guilty about the trouble she'd caused. Then she thought of Indigo and Mary and the rest of the trail of destruction that had come out of the old chain.

"Yes, but they came around. They couldn't disagree with the fact that the message has gotten garbled pretty badly in the past. It probably wouldn't surprise you to know that we recently started a prayer request for a woman named Nancy McReigh, who had a daughter with laryngitis."

Nancy sank back in her chair and closed her eyes. "I was afraid it was something like that," she whispered.

The pastor let the silence hang for a moment. "Yes, and that was the clincher at the meeting. You need to know that the prayer chain members felt awful about what your family went through."

"It wasn't their fault."

"Mmm. Probably not."

She leaned forward and propped her hand on her chin. "But Dave, why? Why did it happen? Why did…"

"Why did God let it happen?"

"Yes."

"I don't know. We may never know."

"That's not good enough for me."

"Well, maybe he needed to teach us something. I got to thinking about the Lord's Prayer, that Jesus taught his disciples to pray. Even though it's full of petition—give us bread, and the rest—the first words are, 'your will be done, on earth as it is in heaven.' And Jesus himself, when he's facing torture and a painful death on the cross, asks his father in heaven to change the rules, to 'take this cup from me.' I can relate to that, it really shows his human side. But then he says, 'not as I will, but as you will.' So even though he's very clear about what he wants, in the end even he surrenders his will. It seems like a powerful lesson for us."

"But you're still doing the prayer chain, or your teleprayer or whatever you call it."

"Yes, but we agreed to begin and end every prayer with thanks to God, and with the words, 'your will be done.' I guess it's just a better way to do it."

"So we just have to trust God, huh?"

"Sure. In the end, that's all we <u>can</u> do anyway, when you think about it. We might as well put our heart into it."

The phone rang and the secretary answered it. "It's Moira, calling about the music for Sunday," she called through the door.

"Tell her I'll call her right back," the pastor said.

Nancy stirred in her chair, figuring it was time to leave.

"But there's another possibility," he said.

"What's that?"

"Well, maybe the whole thing didn't have anything to do with us at all. Maybe we were caught in the middle of something else, like in the book of Job. Maybe it was some kind of cosmic struggle, and we were just caught in the crossfire."

Nancy felt herself shiver. "You don't really think so, do you?"

"I don't know. It could be the case, though."

She thought about it for a moment. It didn't seem like a very satisfying answer; the universe should be more understandable than that.

"And there's one more possibility," he said quietly. "It all may have been for your benefit."

"For my benefit? In what way?"

"Well, you're here, aren't you? You came to church on Sunday."

"Oh no, don't pin it on me. Too many people were hurt by it."

"Yeah, but it got your attention, didn't it? And there wasn't any real lasting damage."

She shook her head. "No, I don't buy it. It affected too many people. And Flip Flaskerud's father even died. I can't imagine God doing that."

"Oh? People die every day, for Mr. Flaskerud it was just a matter of when. But the question for you is, do you think that God cares enough about you to go to those lengths?"

"Well, no, I don't."

"All right, then listen to this." He reached behind to his desk and picked up a Bible. He thumbed through it, looking for a passage. "Here it is. 'If a man owns a hundred sheep, and one of them wanders away, won't he leave the ninety-nine on the hills and go to look for the one that wandered off? And if he finds it, I tell you the truth, he is happier about that one sheep than about the ninety-nine that didn't wander off.'" He closed the Bible and looked at her. "Don't you think it's possible that Jesus is talking about you in that passage?"

"No, he's talking about sheep."

"It's a parable. A metaphor."

"Yeah, I guess I knew that." She thought about the image, about a shepherd searching for a sheep lost in a canyon. She wasn't sure she could accept that it applied to her, but the thought was comforting.

She stood up. "By the way," she said, "did the prayer chain have any kind of prayer for someone named Wayne a while back—say, two months ago?"

He rubbed his forehead. "Wayne, Wayne. Let's see." He stood up too, thinking. "Yes, now that you mention it. Wayne Shoemaker. He's an older member of our congregation. Had an accident, we prayed for healing. Why?"

"Let me guess. He fell, didn't he? When he had his accident."

"Uh, yeah. Didn't break anything; we were afraid he'd broken his pelvis or something. How did you know?"

"And the other day, at the hospital. Bruce asked you—sort of as a joke—to have your congregation pray for the sun to come out, or something like that. You did it, didn't you?"

He chuckled. "Yes, I'll admit it. We used it as the first test of the teleprayer gizmo there. I figured we couldn't go wrong—God probably gets a billion prayers about the weather every day anyway." Revelation swept across his face. "Oh, I get it! Praying for Wayne falling turned into rain falling, and it kept going until we asked it to stop. Something like that?"

She shrugged. "Could be."

"Well, we'll never know. And maybe the real secret is that our second prayer ended with the words, 'not my will, but your will.' Ultimately, we have to surrender our lives into his hands. Do you know what I mean?"

"Yes," she said quietly. "Even this lost sheep is starting to figure that out."

17

A week of sunshine had done wonders for the plants. Lawns that were normally brown and dormant in late July were dark green and growing out of control. Marigolds seemed to double in size each day, and on her walk to work, Nancy noticed that almost overnight the fluorescent pink of wave petunias had grown to completely carpet a hillside.

Sitting at the table in the kitchen, she made a list for the supply order she would need to make—it had become a daily chore now—and then entered yesterday's receipts into her account balance. She had been able to catch up with all the past due charges from her vendors, and still have plenty of money to cover the bank loan at the end of the month.

The infusion of tourist traffic had made a huge difference, but that alone didn't account for the jump in business. Somehow, the line of cars parked along the curb in front of the café had caught the attention of the locals, and even they had been coming in record numbers. The lunchtime crowd was consistently filling the place to capacity, and it was all she could do to take the orders and help Mary with the salads and other side dishes. She had put a sign over the coffee pots and water pitchers, inviting customers to help themselves with refills since she and Jaime weren't getting to them in time. Instead of balking at the self-service, people actually seemed to like it—it made the place seem homier.

To get caught up, Nancy had to work a little later each day, and the housework was beginning to suffer. Bruce hadn't said anything about it, but he spent a good part of his evenings cleaning up the kids' clutter and it seemed she hardly saw him.

From her purse she pulled a piece of paper with the phone number for a woman who did housekeeping. She called the number and the woman answered on her cell phone. She was available two afternoons a week, which would allow the children to go home earlier than usual. They made arrangements to meet that evening at Nancy's house.

Nancy sat back in her chair. The café was quiet except for the hum of the refrigerators and the low rumble of cars and trucks on the street outside. She could afford the housekeeper now, but what if her business slowed down again? And it looked like she needed a backup cook for busy evenings. The money was there now, but she didn't want to have to hire someone and then turn around and lay her or him off when the money got scarce.

She remembered the quote that Dave Montgomery had read on Sunday: Don't worry about tomorrow; tomorrow will worry about itself.

***

By mid morning the café was already half full, but the customers were mostly drinking coffee and didn't take much work. Isaac came bounding in, his thick gray hair shimmering in the sunlight. He slid onto a stool at the counter.

"How about this weather, huh?"

"Yeah. But I didn't think you would be happy

about it," Nancy said.

"Why's that?"

"I thought you introspective artist types preferred gloom and clouds. You know, to bring out the angst, or whatever you call it."

"Well, I don't know about the angst, but the weather brought out the tourists. I sold a dozen paintings last week."

"Wow! I hope you didn't sell the one of the dogs playing poker."

"Oh? You should have told me you wanted it. I thought a velvet Elvis was more to your taste."

Nancy laughed. "Seriously, I'm glad you had a good week."

"Yeah, let me tell you how good it was."

As Isaac talked, Nancy kept an eye on her customers. "Hold on just a second," she said, and carried a pot of coffee around the tables, filling the cups that were empty.

"I thought it was self-service now," Isaac said after Nancy slipped the pot back onto the warming plate.

"Yeah, when it's busy, but I still prefer the personal touch."

"Plus you can eavesdrop on the conversations."

"I wouldn't do that!"

"Yeah, right."

"But now that you mention it, I wonder who Jaime's talking to over there."

Isaac stiffly turned sideways in his stool so he could look out of the corner of his eye. "Can't say I know her. Of course, all that means is that she doesn't appreciate fine art."

"You mean she doesn't want to pay money for

paint-by-numbers water colors."

"Ha ha."

The girl looked to be in her early twenties, with a long blond ponytail and wearing a T-shirt and overalls that only partly hid the curve of her hips. She wasn't eating or drinking anything, and Jaime--only a few days out of his cast--didn't seem to be in a hurry to take her order. Instead, he leaned against a chair next to her, deep in conversation. Isaac turned back and launched into a story of a customer who came in to buy a painting, but liked the frame better than the picture. Always vigilant for an opportunity to make money, Isaac had popped the painting out and sold the frame at a 100% markup.

Jaime finally stood up. "Who's your customer?" Nancy asked him before he could slip into the kitchen.

"Her? Oh, that's Renee. I've actually had the pleasure of spending the last several evenings with her," he said, winking at Isaac.

"That so?" Isaac said. Nancy just smiled.

"As a matter of fact, yes. Her grandfather is at the same nursing home as my grandma. We're trying to match them up," he said, and disappeared through the door.

"Nursing home? What's that about?" Isaac asked.

"It's a long story."

"Well, it'll have to wait. I've got to get back to the shop. Thanks for the coffee." He left a dollar on the counter.

***

Nancy was in the kitchen, ladling a bowl of soup, when Jaime told her that Katharine was in front and needed to talk to her. She carried the soup out, and topped off the water glasses, then went behind the counter to brew up some fresh coffee.

"So. What's up?"

Katharine had her chin propped in her hand and hardly looked up. "I got a call from the prayer chain last night. Prayer machine, I should say."

"Yeah. So?"

"So the prayer request freaked me out."

"Go on."

"It was a request to pray for my job," she said. Nancy could barely hear her over the other conversations in the room.

"*Your* job? I don't get it."

"Neither did I. But I got to work this morning, and

Marge said I was fired. Just like that. Out of a job."

"Are you kidding? Why? How could she do that?"

"Because of this." Katharine pulled a milk glass bowl from her purse. She turned it over. The price tag read $255.95. "Marge said that she lost a sale because of this. The customer was so outraged at the price she said she would never step foot in the store again. I told Marge that I didn't remember putting that price on it, but it was with all the other ones that I had priced. She said I was either lying, or too careless in my work. Either way, she said she couldn't afford an employee like that."

Nancy fell into the chair behind the counter. "Oh no," she said.

"That's what I thought."

"But Katharine, I'm the one who wrote that price on it."

Katharine looked up, startled.

"You did? How."

"When I was up there asking about the prayer chain. You left to go find a phone number. The pen was just sitting there..." Nancy buried her head in her hands. "I'm so sorry."

"It's okay."

Through a haze, Nancy had a dim perception of the room filling up with the early lunch crowd, with a happy noise of laughter and friendly conversation. A moment ago it would have been a welcome sound; now it seemed out of place. She slowly looked up and watched as a sunburned group of college students--probably white water rafters--took a table.

Then she noticed that Katharine had turned away and seemed to be trying to suppress a grin. "By the way, the answer is yes."

"The answer to what?" Nancy asked.

"You asked if I was kidding. Maybe it was a rhetorical question, but the answer is yes, I was. I guessed you had put that price on the bowl."

"You mean you still have your job?"

"Yep."

"Oh! Thank God."

"Yes," Katharine said, and touched Nancy's elbow. "I do. Every day."

www.ingramcontent.com/pod-product-compliance
Lightning Source LLC
Chambersburg PA
CBHW070504120726
47910CB00003B/1119